Chaos & Clover

by

Kandi Silvers

Chapter One

"Just what the hell is that supposed to mean?" Nashville O'Leary directed his temper at the black phone set to the speaker on his dark, expensive mahogany desk.

"It means I'm done, Nash," his father grumbled from the other end of the phone.

Here we go again!

Rolling his eyes, he noticed Julie walk by in a short skirt that barely covered her behind. She honestly had the nicest legs in the office. He glanced at the low-cut white blouse. The flimsy fabric exposed her cleavage he had encountered intimately, more than once.

"I can only imagine." His dad's tone revealed he was downright pissed with every word spoken. "Instead of running that company, you're busy spending time with the female employees in your office in positions that have nothing to do with work and everything to do with satisfying your desires."

Fuming, Nash pulled his gaze from the view of Julie's firm ass in the contours of her skirt and refocused on the phone. "I don't spend time with them in my office."

"But, you spend work time looking and planning how to get them into the bedroom. Nash, the time has come. Your sales are horrible, and I refuse to lose another penny because instead of acting like a CEO, you insist on being a teenager on a sexual rampage. I've made up my mind."

Don't sell the company, please, don't sell the company.

"I'm selling the company. Lucky Ice Cream is going up for sale."

Son-of-a-bitch! This was worse than not good —more like horrific.

"Tell me what you want me to do, and I'll do it." Nash reached for the tie around his neck and pulled on it as if loosening a noose.

His father chuckled. He obviously liked the sound of those words. "Stop pulling on that tie of yours. It's worth more than what some of our secretaries make daily."

Wondering if there were cameras, he glanced around and resented that remark.

Hell!

Nash admitted he resembled the statement.

"The sale of the company can be avoided if you increase the sales in the company over the summer."

"Thank you, Dad. I'll make every sunshine-filled day count."

"You're damn right you're going to make them count—even if you are going to be a sarcastic ass.

Not only will you make my company successful, but you will also provide me with a grandchild."

He wanted to protest. Instead, his words caught in his throat. Nash started coughing loudly, hoping to dislodge the invisible tennis ball cutting off the air to his lungs. Maybe death had finally found him.

He thought of more sinful ways to die and decided he better live now. "I have no intentions of burdening myself with one woman every day for the rest of my life. I'm a buffet sort of guy, Dim Sum even, as opposed to a favorite meal."

"Nash!" his father bellowed.

This was not the time to discuss the fact he had no intentions of ever getting married. "Dad..."

"I'm not asking you to marry someone. I still wonder why I married your mother."

"I heard that Charlie!" his mother yelled from somewhere in the background.

Tension built around his head. There were days he wasn't strong enough to deal with Monica and Charlie O'Leary.

"Damn that woman. I ask her for a clean shirt, and she doesn't hear me."

"About the baby thing, I'm not getting married."

"As I was saying before, your mother started squawking. I said nothing about a wife. I simply want you to find a nice girl. Do what you do. It's not hard. Think like you always do, and it should be a snap. I'll have a grandchild in the works by month's end."

The tension in Nash's head turned into a migraine. "Is there anything else before I have my morning board meeting?"

"Yes. I have a new Advertising Executive, Clover Callaghan, to help you. Be nice, and don't hit on her, for Christ's sake. That will be all. Have a good meeting."

"What happened to Davis in advertising?"

"He quit last month after your rendezvous in the mailroom with his wife from accounting."

"Sharon hit on me."

"Have a good day, son." His father ended the call with, "Be nice to Ms. Callaghan, but not too nice."

Pressing the button on the phone, Nash furrowed his brows. His father was being unreasonable. He could avoid the sale of the company. He was Ivy League educated. Of course, he could. The baby part was a problem.

Sure, lots of women he could get to do the deed, just none he wanted to be tied to with a child. Marriage or not, he would have to deal with the baby's mother from time to time. He sighed in defeat, pulled open his top drawer, and removed the bottle of acetaminophen.

He quickly removed the lid, shook two, and popped them back. Putting the cover back on, he regretted the decision to skip water as they lodged themselves halfway down his throat. On the bright side, the tennis ball had again vanished, so he could partially breathe except for now heavy weight on his chest.

The tablets started to dissolve. He scrunched his face at the bitterness. It was beginning to feel like a Monday. Too bad it was Friday.

Chapter Two

Clover Callaghan was late. She shouldn't have gone surfing before work, but the waves were too good to resist. Now she was scrambling through LA traffic to the Lucky Ice Cream headquarters and offices. She still couldn't believe she had taken an actual job, unlike the consulting she preferred. It wasn't like she needed the money, and the nine-to-five routine cut into perfect surf time.

She thought of Charlie, her father's longtime friend, and his sweet wife Monica, who shared her mother's love for flowers. Poor Charlie had almost begged and pleaded for her to save the struggling ice cream company that his playboy son was running into the ground. She scrunched her face as she brought her Lexus SUV to the parking garage of the office tower.

What did she know about Nashville O'Leary? Nash was hot when he was seventeen, he kissed really well, from what she recalled, and he liked women that put out. Even though kissing him at the country club on the green of the fifteenth hole the summer she was sixteen didn't amount to anything, she didn't put out.

Their encounter was short-lived when her cousin Patrice bragged how he had ended up with his pants down and giving her a *hole n' one* two days later. That was the end of Nashville O'Leary. After all, a girl had to have standards, and Clover had hers.

It worked out in the long run. Clover returned to Houston to her private girl's school, then went to the University of Florida to be closer to her family. Even when Charlie and Monica O'Leary moved out to Orlando, she didn't recall Nashville ever coming for a visit. She scowled.

I hope I've outgrown him.

She pulled the silver Lexus into a parking stall and paused. Anxious butterflies fluttered in her stomach. She hated being nervous. She grabbed her knapsack and shut the door. Her surfboard was in the back, and she had already experienced withdrawal. Catching her reflection in the tinted window, she thought for a moment and glanced at her clothes. The other downside to nine-to-five was the attire, which currently hers didn't suit.

If the corporate world spent a little more time out of their high-rise towers and more time barefoot on the beach, cut-offs would be perfectly normal wear. Too bad for Nashville O'Leary. Today they were.

Nashville!

With her knapsack flung over her shoulder, she walked to the elevator and pushed the button. Maybe he wasn't good-looking anymore. Perhaps he was ugly now and forty pounds overweight.

Could I be so lucky?

Not that ugly or fat suited the playboy image, unless he was a pimp and wore heavy gold chains around his neck, cheesy off-colored suits, and his hair slicked back into a ducktail. Again, it wasn't a sexy thought but one that eliminated the jitters in her stomach.

He wasn't a pimp, though. He was the CEO of a company running into the ground from being well—for lack of a better phrase—a male slut. She groaned. He couldn't be that spectacular; after all, he was single.

She scrunched her features as she walked onto the elevator, and the doors closed. Punching the number to the twenty-fifth floor, it dawned on her that she was also single—only because her surfboard had more intelligence than most men. Boy's brains were in their balls; that's where they slipped during puberty and never found the energy to relocate above the shoulders again.

It was sad, really. A travesty.

How they ever made it past the ape stage was a miracle. Men were proof that not all species evolved.

The elevator stopped, and she stepped off into the luxurious lobby. Everything was posh and sophisticated.

This is bad.

Clover stuck out more than a white body on a suntanned beach. She was tanned but way underdressed. A woman walked by and gave her the once-over, then blanched. Okay, so maybe the cut-offs and Hello Kitty T-shirt weren't the best fashion choices—or the fact that the ties to her two-piece swimsuit peeked out at the neck. Oh well, she was here now.

She approached the receptionist, who was literally gawking at her. Her mouth parted, her eyes peered over her glasses, and her coiffed hair was perfectly in place. Her sweater was draped over her shoulders and held together with a sweater clip. Once Clover moved past all thoughts on the woman's hair, she was sure the sweater clip would fetch a reasonable price at a retro kiosk on the beach. "Hello."

"I'm sorry, dear. We aren't giving out any donations right now."

Don't be rude. Just breathe.

"I'm Clover Callaghan, the new advertising executive, not some bum, so why don't you play secretary and tell me where I can find Nashville O'Leary's meeting." She flashed a smile and decided not to be *too* rude. Judgmental people grated on her nerves. It was up there with animal cruelty and sticky floors.

The older woman's brows shot up. Her thin lips were pursed together, almost making them totally disappear. "I'm sorry, the large oak doors on your right down the hall. Is there anything I can get you, Ms. Callaghan?" Her attitude had changed.

"No, that's fine…." She lifted the nameplate off

the desk. “Sally. Thank you.”

“Well, if there is anything I can do to help.”

“Well,| Clover debated as she turned away. “You can stop kissing my ass any time.”

Yep, it was going to be a good day after all.

Chapter Three

Nashville's headache had not improved fifteen minutes into his meeting, and most of his staff were nimrods. The highlight was the flash of Julie's cleavage as she shifted in her seat while taking notes. His father had hired some woman to take over in a vital department of this company, and she didn't have the decency to get here on time. What the hell? Why was he worried about the company?

He had more severe problems—the whole baby thing, for example. He stole a sideways glance at Julie. She certainly wasn't maternal, and he couldn't imagine his child being raised by her.

The band around his head tightened further, his headache escalating to migraine.

Lovely.

He leaned his head into his hand. As Nash doodled on the notepad in front of him, his elbow propped the desk for support while Fritz from accounting went over the sales dollars.

It was as bleak as his chance as a child.

Neither of the two he really wanted to think about. However, thanks to his dear old dad, his thoughts now thrust into those dark, shark-infested waters. Save the company from the sale and a child. That was damn near blackmail and caused his grip to tighten on his pen.

The heavy oak door opened, and the room fell quiet. Fritz had finally shut up about the sad situation of finance and turned his head toward the door. Sally better have food or a Valium that would knock out a horse for his headache.

What the hell?

His elbow slipped off the table and jarred his head. He focused on long, tanned legs and sat upright in his chair. The legs were tucked under frayed short cut-offs and curved over hips that narrowed at the waist. Her white T-shirt fit tight against her body.

Nash's gaze dipped over full breasts strained against the T with a kitty on it, and his groin stirred to the point it strained against his pants.

Someone should have told the new arrival not to wear a black bra beneath a white shirt, but his eyes continued ascending to the doll-like face. Strawberry blonde hair in two pigtails framed a tanned nose with freckles, and big brown eyes peeked from between the longest lashes he had seen.

He blinked. It wasn't a black bra; it was a swimsuit.

His mind registered the detail, taking in the chunky yet practical sandals and the knapsack slung over her shoulder. She looked entirely out of place, but his body argued that place should be on him, straddling his lap, to be more specific. He couldn't stand in the lady's presence. The little CEO in his pants was as stiff as a board, so that wasn't an option. He waved her in further.

Her full mouth formed an "oh," which wasn't what Nash needed. "I'm sorry, are you lost?"

She blinked, glanced to the door that shut tight, and looked back at him, dazed. "Evolution," she murmured.

Was she ill? It didn't matter. She was turning him on.

"Evolution? As in Darwin?" he asked, not having time for the distraction. Why had he asked? He was just encouraging the crazy beach bum. She was a long way from the sandy shores currently.

"Darwin, apes, species." She shook her head and stepped further into the room.

"Can I help you?"

With more than seeing what the rest of that swimsuit looks like?

She smiled warmly, and he hoped it got better than this, so he could send her on her way. He frowned. There was something strangely familiar about her.

"Nashville O'Leary—I'm Clover Callaghan, your new advertising executive."

"Screaming fucking hell!"

His directors gasped. He hadn't meant to say it aloud, only think it, but she was not dressed for an office, and she was the last thing his libido needed exposure to.

Things hadn't gotten better. They had gotten worse in record time. She wasn't executive material, but with his hard-on from hell, she might just be his baby's mother.

"Everybody out!" he barked. Clover turned. "Oh no, not you, Ms. Callaghan. Everyone else!"

Her big brown eyes widened, and long lashes blinked. "So, this how it's going to be?"

He had no idea what she was talking about, but once the blood returned from his cock to his brain, he might have an answer.

Chapter Four

Clover didn't dare move. Nashville looked pissed.

His staff scampered out of the room like kicked puppies. One woman in a short black skirt paused, scowled a look of disapproval in Clover's direction, and walked out the door with more sway of her ass than required. She was the last to leave, and the door shut tight behind them, leaving Clover alone with the seething hunk.

The son of a bitch couldn't have gotten ugly, fat, or even bald. No, not my luck. He's hotter than hell.

Her swimsuit soaked between her legs. It had nothing to do with her earlier wave-catching and everything to do with the yummy male in Armani across a big table from her. She furrowed her brows. He still hadn't stood.

Apparently, he didn't have Charlie's manners.

Nashville placed both elbows on the table and buried his face in his hands. Not the reaction she was going for, but okay, she was a professional. She could work with it. "Are you all right?"

Lifting his head slightly, he peered over his fingertips and laughed as if she had said something funny. "No!" It was a whimpering sound.

I wonder if the CEO's mental health is part of the company's problem.

Her brows furrowed. This was turning out rather unusual. She cleared her throat. "Can I get you anything?"

"Can you get me anything?" His tone was off, but she guessed so was the man himself. He rubbed his hand across his forehead and shook his head.

She debated. "Do you want something for your headache?"

Nash shook his head. "Not unless you have Valium."

She stepped closer to him. "I don't do drugs. I prefer natural remedies."

He lowered his hands and narrowed his gaze on her. "Natural remedies? Like your outfit as opposed to a suit and nylons?"

"Nylons are for bank robbers and should only be worn over the head." She smiled at her comeback.

"You seem familiar. Have we met?"

He doesn't remember me. Why would he? I didn't give him a hole-in-one.

"I know your father; he's good friends with my father."

The proverbial lightbulb went on above his head, and his brows lifted. "You're Mighty Mickey's daughter." The gesture was short-lived as he closed his eyes and groaned. "Of course…."

Pain marred his features, and he sat back in his chair. He pinched the bridge of his nose and glanced back at her. "You're the wild one."

Do not be offended and hostile.

"You're a ruthless playboy running your dad's company into the ground, and you call me wild?"

Not what I was going for, but it's already said, and the damage is done.

His brows shot up. "I'm also your boss."

"Who isn't doing an outstanding job at running this company."

"Tell me, would that be a professional opinion, or did a seashell at the beach tell you that."

Wow, what a sarcastic ass, so much for not being rude. How does this guy bang babes like a construction worker does nails with a hammer?

Some things were better left unanswered. "We seem to have gotten off to a rough start."

"Clover, I—"

"You what, Mr. O'Leary?"

He sighed and leaned closer to her again. "Please take a seat." He waved to a chair where the blonde, who'd given her a dirty look, had sat. She sat and crossed her legs, sending sand to slide out of her shoe. He inhaled deeply, held his breath, and stared at the sand on the rich navy carpeting.

His gaze lifted, dragging up her legs and body until her body hummed. She was more than aware he had just checked her out. "You just got sand on the floor." His tone was calm and even disdainful, but his eyes sparked with lust.

Her pussy twitched at the thought. "Well, you're very observant." That was a compliment.

"I'm very observant. You have a great set of legs, Ms. Callaghan, but tomorrow I want to see them tucked under a skirt and a proper shirt. Also, we are nowhere close to the beach, so there is no need to wear a swimsuit under your clothes. The sprinkler system is fine, so don't consider it an excuse."

He noticed my legs but was babbling like an idiot.

Despite being hot, Nashville O'Leary was an odd duck. Kind of like his aunt Wilma. "Did I do something to offend you?"

He paused and blinked. "My father has sent you to spy on me and prove that I can't run this company. Of course, I find you offensive."

Whoa! Where did that come from?

Clover shook her head while she weighed and measured her following words. "That's not entirely true."

He tilted his head, and his dark brown eyes penetrated her soul. Her breath caught. She didn't think he was out to seduce her, but he looked sexier than sin, and sin was what was crossing her brain.

"Are you saying I'm wrong, Ms. Callaghan?"

"Call me Clover, and as a matter of fact, I am." Her gaze locked with his, and her cheeks heated despite the fight against her attraction. She was blushing.

His lashes flickered several times quickly to reveal a stunned expression on his face. "No one tells me I'm wrong."

"Well, get used to it." She smiled. "On the bright side, we just experienced our first—first."

"First—first, that makes no sense."

"Neither does your level of anxiety. I can dress more office appropriate if it will appease you."

Nashville O'Leary's mouth dropped open, still sexy but slightly caveman-like in thinking. It was hard to believe she thought he had evolved into a man. Sadly, he had the body of a man—a vast body built for pleasure type of man—but had an extreme case of brains in the balls disorder.

Clover couldn't resist the comment. "What now? Are you more shocked I knew the word *appease* or used it correctly?"

"Do you insist on speaking your mind?"

She rolled her eyes and wished she had brought Legos or a coloring book and crayons to amuse the little boy in the man suit. "You're nothing like I remember. I'm not sure why I told your father I'd take this job. You're out of control and need help. I can't give you the kind of help—more like a padded room and a great white coat—extra-long in the sleeves."

"I'm not crazy," he replied tersely.

Clover studied him intently and didn't believe his last statement. "Then why are you giving me such an attitude?"

He paused and finally stood. Pacing the room, he looked at Clover and shoved his hands into his suit pockets. "I only found out this morning you were coming."

"Surprise?" she offered with a weak smile and slightly shrugged. Clover wasn't sure what to think or feel.

"I hate surprises."

Did he have to say that through gritted teeth?

It was a shame it was almost March because he had the whole Grinch thing nailed, or maybe it was Scrooge. It didn't matter; he wasn't exactly Mr. Warm Hospitality with congeniality sprouting out of his mouth and ass.

No, but a pole up his ass is a possibility.

"I'll show you to your office, then you're excused for the rest of the day until tomorrow. You will be here at eight a.m. sharp, without your current outfit and the stowaway sand. You'll be dressed as an executive, and we'll all move forward. Any questions?"

Don't say it, don't say it.

"Will you have had an enema by then? Because, frankly, whatever you have lodged up your ass needs to come out."

Damn! I said it.

"You're impossible." Nashville O'Leary scowled.

"And you can't do much about it since your daddy sent me." Clover smiled in victory.

Nash narrowed his gaze, and a bizarre thing

happened. He smiled. Not only did he have a great smile, but he also had really nice teeth. Gorgeous. With his clean-cut hair and crisp suit, he could have stepped off any hoity-toity magazine cover for men.

"Tell me, Clover, did you remember a resume for my files?"

She breathed. Who knew she had held her breath? "Of course." She reached down, slid a hand inside her backpack, and pulled out the expensive linen paper. Despite her doubts about being there and taking the job, she stood and passed her resume to him. He was a few inches taller.

Nash took it and paused. He lifted it to his nose, and his nostrils flared with an inhale. He lowered the paper and blinked jet-black lashes at her. "It smells like sunblock."

"I have to take care of my skin."

His eyes raked over her blatantly, and for a fraction of a second, desire ignited in his eyes, then vanished. "And I have to take care of my company. You just earned the empty office next to me."

"Wow, favoritism! Won't the other O'Leary groupies be jealous?"

His smile faltered. "I plan on keeping a very close eye on you."

Clover smiled and turned on her heel. "You're the boss!" She walked to the door as his eyes burned against her body. He was checking her out.

"I don't know if I appreciate your candid demeanor," he announced as his footsteps crossed to her in just two strides.

Turning, she fought the liquid mush that had once been her stomach. It was all that remained from girl-like jitters. She tilted her chin. "What don't you appreciate? The fact I'm not intimidated by your looks or the fact that it turns you on?"

His eyes darkened, and his lips curved into another smile. "I refuse to answer that."

She resisted the urge to snort in amusement at his comment. "Thanks, Mr. O'Leary, but you just did."

"Call me Nash."

I would call your name in bed if you wanted.

"Nash it is."

Chapter Five

Charlie O'Leary glanced at the grandfather clock. It was eleven o'clock at night at his home in Florida. The phone started to ring, and he looked at the number. He turned to Mickey Callaghan. Sure enough, it was his son. Nash would be home from work this evening, no doubt moping around his penthouse.

"Is it my daughter or your son?" Mickey smirked and lifted his mug of beer.

"My boy, no doubt phoning to bitch about your daughter." He reached for the phone and grinned. "Hello, Nash. How's my son?"

"Cut the crap, Dad. How the hell do you think I am?"

"I don't know, son. If I knew, I wouldn't have asked." The other line beeped in, and he smiled. "Hang on, Nash, I have to take this." He smiled at Mickey and clicked the line over. "Hello?"

"Charlie, what the hell have you gotten me into?" Clover barked from the other end of the phone. "You never told me Nash was a power-hungry, uptight—"

"I know, dear. It's okay. Hang on just one

moment." He hit the mute button and turned to Mickey. "I owe you five dollars. You're right. They aren't getting along."

"Excellent." He chuckled. "Serves those two kids right."

He clicked off the mute and hit line one. "Sorry, Nash, now where were we?"

"We were nowhere. You sent Clover Callaghan in to spy on me. Dad, how could you? What was all that bullshit on the phone this morning?"

"I don't understand, son. Clover is to help with advertising."

"I read her resume, which, by the way, smelled of sunblock. She has no advertising experience. She has lots of consulting, and I recognize these companies. They are all companies that were reorganized before being sold."

So he thinks he's so bright?

"Hang on, Nash. I have to take a call."

"No, Dad—" Charlie hit the hold button.

"Putting up a bit of a fight, huh?" Mickey chuckled. "Let's see what my daughter has to say."

He hit the button and put Clover on speaker. "Sorry, Clover, I had to deal with just a hostile call."

"Well, to be honest, Charlie, I'm not so sure I won't be *hostile*. Your son put me in the office next to him."

Mickey smiled and nodded. Charlie was pleased. "Well, Clover, what's wrong with that? You are going to be a big part of Lucky Ice Cream."

More than you know.

"Possibly, but I wasn't counting on your son being Dr. Jekyll and Mr. Hyde. One minute he is snapping orders like a mad drill sergeant, and the next, he's looking at me like I'm his favorite ice cream topping."

"Oh, lass, hang on. Have to take another call." He placed the call on hold and laughed. "She certainly has a bee in her bonnet."

Mickey sipped his beer and raised his glass to Charlie. "And your son is obviously attracted to her. "I'll bet you a dollar he hits on her in the next twenty-four hours."

Charlie shook his head. "My son wouldn't dare. I say we make it two dollars."

He slapped his thigh. "Done." He wiggled his brows. "Let's see what Nash is thinking."

"Nash, sorry, important call."

"Who was it?" There was a pause. "You were talking to Clover, weren't you?"

At least he has some brains.

"Yes, she thanked me for the opportunity to work for the company."

"No, she wasn't. She was probably complaining that she couldn't bring her surfboard to the office and what a jerk I was!" Nash fumed.

"No, she likes you, Nash. She had nothing but good things to say about you."

Silence ensued.

"Really?"

So the boy changes his tone.

"Yes." The light went off on line two, and the

phone started ringing again.

No doubt Clover is calling back.

"Nash, hang on." He hit the button. "Hello?"

"Charlie, I need to talk to you about this!" Clover blared over the speaker.

"Hang on, Clover." He hit the button. "Mickey, your daughter has quite the temper. Think she can use it on my son?"

"Won't that just encourage him?"

"If our Irish luck prevails!" He hit the button. "Sorry, Nash. Don't worry about anything; just handle Clover like any other beautiful lady. I have to go." He ended the call and hit the speaker button. "Clover, I have to go. Don't worry about Nash. Just keep that boy in his place and flash him that beautiful smile. He will be eating out of your hand in no time."

Mickey chuckled. He was enjoying this far too much.

"Well, that's great, Dad, but this is Nash!" his son's voice boomed into the room.

Mickey lifted his beer and looked away, his smile gone.

Charlie reached for his mug.

This is going to take more work than I thought.

Chapter Six

Nash was still fuming over the call with his father the night before as he stepped off the elevator. "Good morning, Mr. O'Leary. You look dashing today," Sally greeted, parked in her chair behind reception.

"Good morning, Sally." He was sure that the woman had been the receptionist at Lucky Ice Cream since the beginning of the company. She was quite the ass-kisser but always did a great deal for his ego. Not to mention she was a sweet lady and knew everything. She was his eyes and ears to the company and the employee gossip.

"Is that a new tie? It sure looks spiffy with that shirt."

Spiffy? Typical Tuesday comment.

He was sure the woman had the compliments on a rotating schedule. Monday his hair, Tuesday his tie, Wednesdays his shoes. Thursdays were joyous affirmation days, and Friday—he couldn't remember Friday. "Is Clover Callaghan here yet?"

"Why, yes, sir." She was more than enthusiastic.

What is she not saying?

The elderly secretary nodded her head. Not a hair of her head moved. "She's been here since I arrived at seven this morning. She called a meeting with sales and accounting."

Oh, did she now?

"And where was this meeting held?"

I can't kill the beach bunny.

The older women cast him a puzzled but concerned expression. "Why, the boardroom, of course."

Of course.

He tapped the oak desk with his knuckles. "Thank you, Sally."

He wasn't amused. Who did Clover Callaghan think she was coming in here and talking to his staff without him? He was only the CEO and part-owner of the company. He glanced at his watch; it was quarter to eight. The official meeting, his meeting, was another fifteen minutes away.

As Nash approached the boardroom, his temper increased. It was time that Clover Callaghan found out who was boss. He pushed open the door and came to a halt. Fritz from accounting sat in a chair, as did Martin from sales.

That wasn't what caused his dead stop. It was the pair of long, tanned legs tucked under a short designer suit skirt complete with jacket and teamed with trendy heels. Her strawberry blonde hair fell in soft waves above her shoulders, and she greeted him with a smile. Pushing herself away from the table, she stood and turned to him. "Good morning, Nash."

His eyes swept over her as he forced himself to get his libido in check. However, the lace trim on her silk camisole beneath the blazer was tempting enough for him to pitch more than a tent in his pants. "Good morning, Clover." He rolled her name on his tongue.

She is so damn beautiful.

Nash crossed the floor over to his chair at the head of the table and noticed Clover's designer handbag on the oak surface. He drew the chair out and sat. "Nice purse; however, I sit here. It's part of the luxury of being the boss."

She leaned in and lifted the purse. Doing so granted Nash a full cleavage shot of her breasts pushed up round and filled in a lace bra. His cock stirred. Two minutes in the room with her, he was getting the hard-on from hell again. He slid the wheels of the leather chair closer to the table to cover whatever might spring up.

"I'll keep it in mind." Straightening her body on the turn, not only did he get a whiff of her perfume, he had an incredible view of her ass.

Julie no longer has the best ass and legs category; the new winner is Clover.

The bulge in his pants grew. His mind registered Clover's fragrance, and the summer he was seventeen came to memory. Surely she still didn't wear the same perfume.

She tossed a smile to Martin and Fritz. "Well, gentlemen, I think we will share the decisions we've decided on with the rest of the—"

"What?" Now she was making decisions without his say.

What the hell?

"What, what?"

He flexed his jaw. "What did you make decisions on?"

"Oh!" Her face lit up.

Excellent, the beach bunny had a clue.

"We discussed and finalized some ideas for marketing, advertising direction, and the product."

He gritted his teeth. "There is nothing wrong with the product."

"Says you," she fired at him with a saucy grin.

He pulled his lower lip between his teeth and tried not to notice her perfectly arched mouth that puffed with a come-kiss-me pout.

She is going to be my undoing!

"Forgive me, Nash, but the flavors are a tad... *vanilla.*" She tossed her hair slightly. "Forgive the ice cream pun."

"Well, all final calls about what happens with this company are mine."

"And I'm here to stir things up."

"Stir things up?" He lifted a brow. Somehow, he didn't think that included his cock, but if it was part of the package, so be it.

Chapter Seven

Is this how the man handles every beautiful woman?

The words Charlie had tossed through the phone at her, thinking she was Nash. Boy, Charlie had a lot of nerve! She smiled at Nash. Okay, it was a little forced, but the man would be her undoing. She hadn't counted on him affecting her down to her thong. It didn't matter. A look, the sound of his voice, hell, even his cologne screamed, kiss me, baby.

She was a professional! She could handle this.

Right, fat chance! He is the devil. Sexier than sin, but sin through and through.

"Did you even hear me?" His sexy baritone asked and dampened her thong in the process.

So much for wearing lace underwear.

She shook her head slightly. "I'm sorry, could you repeat that?"

He sighed, and people started to file in. The blonde from yesterday raked her gaze over Clover and scowled, then sat next to Nash in the chair where Clover had sat only a moment or two earlier. Nash's brows went up, and his gaze held fast to

Clover. "I asked what you meant by stirring things up."

Excellent, he didn't get it. Maybe Clover should get a whiteboard and markers. She cleared her throat. "I mean to take charge and fix what's broken."

"Nothing is broken. Now take a seat." Nash pointed to the chair on the other side of him across from the blonde that didn't like her.

What is up with that chick?

She walked over to the chair and stared at Nash. "Well, if the company wasn't broken, why is your father paying me an enormous salary to fix it?"

"Oh dear," someone murmured.

His tongue snaked across his teeth before he set his jaw and donned an unamused expression. "Because my father is old and losing his mind."

"No, Nash. This company is as stagnant as swamp water, and you are the king crocodile in the sludge."

There, that was telling him.

Silence echoed through the room. No one even breathed, she was sure. "I'm here to blow new life into the company. Consider me here to put the *luck* into Lucky."

He rose to his feet and faced her down. "I have the final say on the decisions."

Did he just flare his nostrils?

She smiled sweetly. "And I have changes that need to be implemented."

"Then they will get run past me." He fastened his suit coat up and sat back down. "Now, take a seat."

Clover blinked.

He has quite the set of balls on him. How dare he dismiss me!

The blonde snickered and looked more than triumphant. She leaned into Nash and whispered something.

"Julie, enough!" he warned.

So that was Julie.

When she arrived this morning, she had overheard Martin and Fritz discussing her and her office hobbies. However, Julie wasn't the current problem.

"I told you to take a seat." Nash didn't even look at Clover, which infuriated her almost as much as she was attracted to him.

"I heard you, but I would like to finish what I was saying before I give in to your little power trip."

He focused back on her. "Power trip?"

"You do know what that is, don't you? If not, I will have to consider a whiteboard to draw pictures or maybe hand puppets to help you clarify."

Oh hell, I'm suffering foot in mouth disease here. Mayday! Mayday! The plane is going down.

"Is this about wanting power in my company?"

She decided she probably should stop poking

the bear with a verbal stick and not only weighed but also measured her following statement. "As I recall, most of the shares are held by your father."

He flinched and narrowed his gaze.

Clover expected him to yell, roar, or bark—whatever hunky egomaniac CEOs did. Instead, his gorgeous mouth curved into a grin. "Well then." He turned back to the people seated at the table. "Julie, take notes and email them to me. Ms. Callaghan and I will resume this conversation in my office."

Oh hell! One pending plane crash with lots of flames. So much for the mayday.

He turned back to her and dared to wear the sexy I-want-to-sin smile. Nash waved his hand toward the boardroom door. "After you, Clover."

Oh hell, this can't be good.

She picked up her purse and file and crossed the navy carpeting to the door. Nash reached it before her and pulled open the door.

"Ladies first."

"Thank you." She treaded over the threshold and stepped closer to her impending doom.

Nash exited behind her and smiled as they walked toward his office. "Won't this be fun?"

Yeah, as exciting as a paper cut.

Chapter Eight

Nash shut his office door behind her and turned. She stared at him with contempt. Her arms folded across her chest did nothing except push her already perky breasts up and to his attention. Like he needed the incentive! "You're out of control."

"Actually, Nash, I am trying to get a little out of your power-hungry hands."

He set his jaw. "If you want power in the company, I'll give it to you. After you marry me and own shares, it will be."

Clover blinked. "You've got to be kidding me." She stepped closer and furrowed her perfectly arched brows. "Yesterday, I thought you had a mental illness. Now I'm unsure if you are on drugs or bipolar."

Bipolar? Drugs? She has a lot of nerve!

He disregarded his thoughts and focused back on the topic at hand. "Don't look so shocked. It's a perfect solution to our situation."

"We don't have a situation, Nash."

He grinned and sat in the chair behind his desk. Clover was hotter than hell when her temper sparked in her eyes. "Yes, Clover, we do." He grinned. "You want to have power in this company and take it in a direction I disagree with. I need to give my father a grandchild. Marry me, and we both win!"

"Marry you?" She rubbed her temples. "As in wedding, bride, and bouquets?"

"Surely you've caught a bouquet at a wedding?" Nash studied her pretty features.

"I have avoided bouquets like I would a hot fiery chunk of meteor plunging toward the earth. Both mean quick and undeniable death." Clover's determined smile was all business.

He lifted his brows at her analogy. "Nicely put. Clover, I'm not asking you to sleep with me. Hell, we don't even have to get married."

She exhaled a slow, drawn-out breath and glanced at the ceiling before returning her gaze to him again. "Reassuring thoughts on both counts."

"I'm only asking you to have my baby."

Clover frowned, and she shook her head. "Last time I checked, that involved naked bodies, sweat-soaked sheets, and a condom-free environment."

Chuckling, he lifted his brows. Heat coursed through him at the image Clover had just conjured up in his mind. The thought of burying his cock deep inside her made his groin grow hard with arousal. It was good that he sat at his desk; it covered the bulge in his suit pants.

"As wonderful as that image would be to share with you." He couldn't erase the image of her in his arms while he brought their bodies to a climax. "I won't push my luck."

"Smart man!" she snapped with the fakest smile Nash had ever seen—beautiful but fake.

"Technology has come a long way. It'll take an hour, maybe two depending on the paperwork. All it takes now is a clinic, a little encouragement from you in a private room so the wild man's army can be placed carefully into their plastic submarine, a quick injection from the doctor into depths unknown, and *we* are in business." Nash was quite pleased with his comeback.

He was even happier with the shock on Clover's face.

Finally. No smart-mouthed comeback.

"Wow! Put like that, it makes me want to do one of two things. I just can't decide if I want to walk off a pier into shark-infested waters or stab myself in the ears with those pencils on your desk just so I don't have to listen to another word that leaves your mouth."

He was speechless. Did Clover forget he was her boss? "That was harsh!"

Her temper sparked in her dark chocolate-colored eyes. "To think I'm just getting started."

His confidence weakened as he removed his gaze from her and stared at the pencil holder on his desk. "Women love me," he muttered, more for his own benefit. He glanced back up at her. "You used to love me, worshiped the ground I walked on!"

"Well, Mr. O'Leary, I don't love you now. Come to think of it, I didn't love you then. You were the kid of my dad's friend. It was nothing past a teenage crush. I don't even really like you if the truth is known. I mean, past how hot you look in your designer suits." Her icy tone and bland undercurrent weakened more of his confidence. The woman was an ego-slashing samurai.

Nevertheless, she thinks you look hot in your suits; imagine what she would say once she had you out of them?

Nash grinned. "So you think I'm hot?"

Clover cast him a sympathetic look. "Yes, and I think it's a shame it goes to waste on such an egotistical, womanizing jerk."

Running his tongue over his lip, he studied the crisp expensive designer suit and how it clung to Clover's shapely body. The girl had definitely grown up and had grown quite the attitude. She cleaned up quite nicely now that she dressed professionally and not as a beach hippie. "Please, Clover, tell me how you really feel."

"By all means, you're the boss. You also think that any woman with good looks lacks brains, and you really can't think past the little executive in your pants." She hadn't even hesitated in her comment.

He couldn't believe this. Nash was more than aware Clover had a brain. She was beautiful, had brains, and had more attitude than his libido could handle. Making a baby with Clover Callaghan the old-fashioned way would be an erotic delight. "Well, since that's how you feel, I'll make this easy." He had the perfect plan. "Marry me and give me a child, or you're fired."

Her eyes widened in shock, and her lips parted in surprise. Nash had won! He could almost taste victory, but what he wanted to taste was her lips.

"Really? Well, that's easy, especially since you can't fire me. Only your dad can. I quit." She turned on her heel and walked towards his office door.

She can't quit.

He needed her and not just at the office. There was no way! He rose from his desk and, in a fluent movement, came between the lovely lady and his office door. "Don't quit!"

"Move! I have an office to clean out." Her voice was firm, but an emotion he couldn't identify flashed across her pretty face.

They were less than a foot apart. From this distance, he could smell her expensive fragrance. "You still wear the same perfume?" He'd meant it as a thought, but it fell to his tongue.

Her slender neck moved as she swallowed. Her chin tilted up. "Don't even...."

"Don't even what? Tell me, Clover, do you not want me to remember, or do you not want this conversation?"

"I want you to move, Nashville O'Leary. I'm quitting, and nothing you can say will change my mind." Her voice had a business tone, but her eyes didn't hold the same assurance.

Weighing her words, he thought back to when they were younger. He had liked her then, and he wanted her more now. "Fine, Clover, have it your way."

Nash stepped, but instead of out of Clover's way, he closed the distance between them and took her slender, curvy frame in the wrap of his arms. His lips came down on hers while her body struggled to escape. He expected more resistance, but as soon he touched the soft fullness of her mouth, he lost himself in her taste.

Instead of her fighting, her lips welcomed his in surprise. He held her closer to him, enjoying the softness of her breasts against his chest. Nash couldn't taste enough of her, so when a small sigh escaped her, he took it as his opportunity to deepen the kiss.

Her tongue met his and beckoned him to probe every inch of her. Desire snaked through him; his cock hardened in pure lust. He slid his hands down her back to her round, firm ass and pressed her against his arousal.

She moaned as he squeezed the flesh in his hands; in turn, she pressed the softness of her pelvis harder against him. His erection, now rock-hard, started to pulse. He deepened the kiss until she finally lifted her lips from his.

Then he noticed her arms had found their way around his neck. She blinked up at him with hesitation; her lips were puffy from the heat of their kiss. "The answer is still no, but I won't quit, only because I like your father—and he's a good friend to my dad."

"Thank you," he rasped out. His breath ragged from the flood of need still pumping through him.

She stepped out of his arms and went to move around him. He caught her gently by the wrist and held her hand to his groin. "You're not going to leave me in this state, are you?"

She giggled, then shrugged. "Why don't you ask Julie to give you a hand with it?" She reclaimed her hand and walked out of his office, shutting the door behind her.

Nash was now not just sexually frustrated, but how did she know about Julie? More so, who else knew? On the plus side, Clover wasn't going anywhere, which meant he hadn't totally lost.

His plan was only delayed.

Chapter Nine

Clover couldn't believe she had the conversation with Nashville that she did. Had he totally lost his mind? Had she lost her mind? Not only had she told him exactly what she thought of him, but she had also kissed him. He was drop-dead gorgeous, affected her libido, and—charming.

The bastard!

The way he had kissed her was indescribable. Never had she experienced a kiss like that, and she somehow doubted she would again. She hurried down to her SUV and paused. She stared at her reflection in the tinted glass and sighed.

I shouldn't have taken this job.

Her mind played with the kiss repeatedly. Clover's body heated and flamed like it had when she had been in his arms, and his lips were to hers. She wasn't sure why he wanted her. So many other women in the office held Nash's eye or had held different parts of his body. She leaned her arms against the side of the vehicle and rested her forehead against them.

Part of her wanted to cry, and the other

wanted to laugh.

Her father wanted her to be responsible; getting married would prove she was. A baby, though? She wasn't ready to settle down, and surfing would be on hold. The beach was her life. Why was she even considering this crazy idea?

Right, her father had accused her of never amounting to anything other than an *educated beach bum*. Playing those words in her mind was enough to break the tie between the laughter and tears and fat water droplets formed on her lashes.

"Clover, I'm sorry if I was out of line."

She lifted her head and lowered her arms from the SUV. She sniffled, turning to look at Nash. "It's okay." Her voice was as watery as her face. She wiped her cheeks with the back of her hand and met his gaze again.

He stepped closer and pulled a crisp handkerchief from his pocket. "Here, I hope those tears aren't because I made you cry."

"Thanks." She took the cloth and dabbed her cheeks. "No, though it was tempting."

His handsome face wore an expression of concern. "Then why the tears?"

"Why me, Nash? We are as opposite as night and day."

He tilted his head to the side and widened his eyes slightly. She knew by his face that he agreed with her on that point. Nash sighed and put his hands in his suit pants pockets. "We are as different as night and day, Clover, and that's okay.

I've dated women like me. They're really shallow."

"So are you." She winced. "I didn't mean that."

He broke into a smile. "Yes, you did!" He removed his hand from the pocket and closed the distance between them. His smile broadened. "It's that disgusting display of saying the first thing that hits your tongue. It's the way you don't stop and care what other people think. You're beautiful, and don't put up with my shit."

She sniffled and patted her eyes again. "What about Julie?"

He ran his tongue over his teeth and looked around the parking garage. He rested his eyes back on Clover. "Can I take you somewhere a little more private, so we can talk?"

Yes. No. Maybe. Dammit! The charming son-of-a-bitch. "I don't know…."

"I promise not to hit on you or make you cry." He withdrew his other hand from his pocket and held both up as if surrendering.

She glanced at the car keys clutched between her fingers and palm, then debated. His hand curled around hers, and she glanced up into his eyes. "Nash…."

"I'll drive, and I will behave. I want to talk." He sighed. "Alone and away from the office."

She wanted to shove him away and climb into her vehicle, but she didn't. She realized that she hadn't retrieved her hand from his either. She nodded her head. "Okay, so help me, Nash, I'll slap you with sexual harassment if you pull a stunt like that again."

She thought of the kiss in the office, and her cheeks burned. Heat darkened Nash's eyes, and though he quickly glanced at her lips, he nodded. At least he understood. She didn't know why she was hoping he would kiss her anyway. "Where did you want to go?"

He smiled and looked sexier than sin. "Where would you be most comfortable?"

She lifted her brows and bit her tongue. Some things were better unsaid.

Chapter Ten

Nash was amazed that Clover never put up a fight over him driving her SUV. He had left his car at the parking garage, a problem he could deal with later, with no clue why he had chased after her. Only Nash hated the way she had left—mad at him. Women were a dime a dozen, but the more he thought about having a baby with Clover, the more the idea seemed promising.

After all, their parents were friends, thus the reason she had ended up at Lucky Ice Cream and thrown his libido way out of whack in the first place. It was also good that the grandparents would be a constant if they weren't together but shared a child.

Did he really want to do the whole fatherhood thing?

No, diapers and crying, teething children were not his idea of a good time. However, the sex involved making one—well, he was good at that.

He didn't know where she wanted to go or where he was driving. The silence between them stretched out. He should say something to her, but what? Starting with the obvious would work.

"Where are we headed to?"

She turned in the seat and looked at him. "Normally, I would say the beach. However, you're not really dressed for it."

"And your Gucci suit is popular sand and surf attire these days?" He shouldn't have been sarcastic, but he honestly couldn't resist.

A weak, halfhearted laugh escaped her. "No. We can go to my place, and I can change. You wanted to talk, so talk."

Right, he had said that.

Stupid, stupid, stupid. Oh, where to begin?

He inhaled a deep breath. "I do feel bad for upsetting you. I only thought that...."

It would be an easy way to get sex out of you and save the company from a sale.

No, that wasn't entirely true either.

"My father told me yesterday that, not in so many words, I had to pull my head out of my ass and use my dick to give him a grandchild. He will sell the company if I don't increase sales and get a grandchild in the oven."

There I said it and sounded desperate in the process. I've never been hopeless. Now, maybe I am.

He shifted his attention slightly from the road and glanced at her. She stared at him as if studying him. Nash focused back on traffic. "You realize that our fathers were together last night, right?"

"Yeah, I figured that. I also know you called when I did. No doubt telling my father what a no good son-of-a-bitch I was."

"I never used those words, but you're close, and you were no doubt whining like a spoiled child over the fact that I was some sort of spy."

"Wow, you're good. Close even. So, now that we have cleared that up, where do you live?"

"Huntington Beach."

"Nice to know you live miles away from the office."

"You couldn't pay me to live in LA."

"I live in LA."

"And I would need to know this. Why?" Her tone was sharp and all too cool again.

This was going to take more work than he had anticipated. "Clover, do you remember the summer when we were younger?"

"Nope!"

She answered too quickly, and he didn't believe it for a second. "I do."

From the rearview mirror, he caught her glance away and out her passenger door window. She was quiet. Why did that make him nervous? He, again, experienced the blow to his confidence. "I remembered your perfume, and I admit that we never really crossed paths, you being out east and me here."

She exhaled a heavy sigh. "Nash, you're babbling. Where is this going?"

"I guess it's because maybe it was a sign that —"

"That you're going to have sex with my cousin on the eighteenth hole again?"

He stopped at a red light that he almost ran. He turned in his seat. "Who was your cousin?"

"Oh, God!" She groaned and covered her face with her hands. "You really have had more women than memory can hold."

"I resent that."

"The word is resembled, not resent." Clover snapped her head in Nash's direction. Her dark eyes held accusation. "But in answer to your question, my cousin Patrice that summer."

He frowned and thought a minute as he stopped at another red light and then turned to face her. "The one with the dark hair?"

Clover slowly nodded her head. "Yeah, that's the one."

She was kidding, right? By the expression on her pretty face, he concluded she wasn't. "Oh please, why would I have had sex with her?"

"Why do you have sex with half the women you do?"

She got me there.

"Because..."

She groaned again and turned away. "How could I even consider this?"

Nash blinked. "You were actually considering my offer?"

"The light is green. Just drive."

"Not until you answer me!" A horn honked behind him.

Her expression was unreadable. "Not until you answer a few questions of mine."

He lifted his foot off the brake and hit the gas.

Oh! Yeah, this is going to take a lot of work.

He reached for his cell phone and called the office. "Yeah, Sally? This is Nashville O'Leary. I won't be in the rest of the day."

"It's illegal to talk on the phone and drive!"

Sighing, he ended the call and shot her a frustrated glance. "So should be your effect on me."

Her eyes widened, and she pivoted her head to stare straight ahead. Nash rejoiced at the moment. It also bought him time to figure out what he would do with the hot strawberry blonde. He wasn't sure if he wanted to choke her or kiss her senselessly. Nash smiled; the latter held more possibilities. He just had to play it cool—a little hard to do when she made him hotter than hell.

Chapter Eleven

An hour later, after spending what felt like forever trapped in a vehicle with Nash, Clover was relieved to be back at her apartment. She changed into a pair of shorts and a T-shirt instead of a suit. Clover entered the living room where Nash had shed his suit, coat, and tie. There he stood with the sleeves of his dress shirt rolled up, studying her bookcase—well, the titles on the books. The man had no right to be so sexy.

Why couldn't he have poorly aged?

He turned and glanced at her. "Interesting choice of books, I'm impressed. I think you have every successful business book ever written." Nash's gaze raked over her legs, then met hers again. His lust was more than apparent.

"I see you made yourself at home," she said, glancing to the back of the plush chair with his coat and tie draped over it. "I somehow don't think you wanted to discuss my choice of reading material."

"No."

She swallowed and wished he didn't affect every nerve in her body. "Have a seat. Do you want a soda?"

"Sure." He sat down on the sofa and looked around the room. "That would be great, as long as it isn't diet."

"I'll see what I can do."

Clover slipped into the kitchen and exhaled the breath she had been holding. She had to get a grip. Swiping two regular sodas out of the fridge, she headed back into the living room and handed him one of the cans.

He smiled and took the can. "I thought it was going to be diet. Thank you."

She sat at the other end of the sofa. "I don't drink diet soda. I don't eat diet food, and I don't worry about fat. I work out pretty hard."

"You have an amazing body. I'm not surprised." The snap of opening his can filled the room. She opened hers and sipped as he undid the top buttons on his shirt.

Okay, go for blunt.

"So, Nash, why me?"

His dark gaze rested on her over the top of his soda can. "Nothing like cutting to the chase and getting to the point."

Clover nodded. "Basically. You'll learn soon enough that's how I work."

"I noticed when I found out you held a meeting without me."

He was infuriating. "I'll send you a formal invite next time."

Nash studied her for a minute. "You have one

hell of an attitude."

"Well, you of all people would be able to recognize the trait in others with the one you carry around."

Wrong words. Damn!

Blinking, he grinned. "There it is—the Callaghan bluntness." He sipped his soda and stared at the can. "I never thought my dad would sell the company or even threaten it."

"Sales are abysmal," she reminded quietly.

He glanced up at her with a solemn look. "I know I can fix it. I'm just not sure how." He shook his head and set the soda can on the coffee table. He stood, shoved his hands in his pockets, and started to pace the floor. "Do you know what it's like to never make your father happy?"

More than you know!

"Parents are tough," she replied flatly. Maybe too flatly. She decided to keep her own parental issues quiet for the moment.

"Right. I know that I have made mistakes, Clover. I'll admit I treated Lucky Ice Cream and the female employees as my playground. I think it's because that's all anyone figured I was capable of."

Don't make me care about you.

His face lit up, and he looked so handsome that she silently called him every evil word. "When I was a boy, I remember going to the office with my dad."

Don't be a happy memory and smile.

His face split into a thong-wetting smile.

Of course, you had to smile. You did that just to annoy me.

She focused on simply breathing in and out and silently repeating how he was not as sexy as she thought.

"I loved going there as a kid. I knew it was cool. I mean, it was great as a kid. My family owned an ice cream company. It made me popular, and from there, I went to playboy. I live in a nice penthouse, drive a Mercedes, and have everything I could want and every toy known to man."

"So, what's the problem?" She tucked her legs up underneath her. "Why me, Nash? Why do you want me to have this baby for you? It's all over the office that Julie and you…."

She wasn't sure how to phrase it eloquently, so she left the statement as-is.

He shook his head, and his expression remained serious. "I admit I had sex with Julie for a while a few months ago, but she is not the kind of person I want to be bound to with a child."

Clover could understand that, but there was still a great deal she didn't. "You don't know me."

"I know how you affect me."

She swallowed hard. Points for him. He actually sounded sincere when he said that.

Okay, too late, I like him.

"Nash," she set her can down and stood. "You realize a baby is a lot of work and—"

"I'm not that clueless. Clover, our parents are friends. If things didn't work between us, it would be okay."

"For who, Nash?" She stepped closer to him. "I have a life, a life I like. However, I'm really questioning this job. You and this crazy baby thing. Not to mention I can surf in Florida. I can go back out to where our families are and explain to your father why I need to quit."

His hand snagged her wrist. "No!" His eyes scanned her face. Her heart picked up speed, and heat moved in flames over her body from his touch. "I know you are attracted to me, Clover."

Lie!

"And don't even think of lying to me."

Suddenly, he was more of an alpha than she knew what to do with, and her breath caught in her throat. "Nash...."

Where the hell is my voice?

"I know you're smart, and if I have to do this parenthood thing and save a company, I know we are compatible." His tone was terse, yet the undercurrent smooth. Her stomach had a nest of butterflies fluttering out of control. His gaze dipped to her lips. She sucked her breath in and closed her eyes to block out the desire burning in his handsome features.

Think!

She swallowed and racked her mind for something logical to stop his effect on her. Everything went blank as his mouth turned hot and hard against her lips. Her lips parted, and his tongue darted over her lower lip, sending a shiver over her entire body.

Clover's nipples hardened, and her tongue met his in hunger. Nash's arm wrapped around her and rested on her lower back, balancing her as his tongue thrust further into her mouth. Instinctively, her hand lifted and rested against his chest.

His grip around her wrist tightened and tugged her gently closer to him. Nash's arm at her lower back pressed her against his groin and the bulge there. Her knees weakened, and she was—what the hell?

She snapped her tongue and lips away and stepped out of his hold. Her breath was ragged, and the most sensual look she had ever seen in a man's eyes stared back at her. She tried to clear her head for coherent thought and failed—miserably.

A wicked smile curved across Nash's lips. "I know you want me as badly as I want you. Try and deny it."

She swallowed and said the first thing that came to her mind. "How about Chinese for lunch?"

His brows shot up, and he nodded, crossing his arms across his chest. "That's what I thought." A thoughtful expression crossed his face. "Chinese sounds good. After we order, you can answer the question I asked you in the vehicle."

"Which was?" At this point, she could barely remember her name, and he wanted her to remember the car ride. Fat chance.

"Were you actually considering my offer?"

She pointed to the phone. "I'll call for that Chinese food."

He chuckled and smiled broadly. "You do that because, sweetheart, I'm not going anywhere until you say yes."

"To beef and broccoli?"

Yes, that's it. Play dumb.

Nash looked like a cat with a bird in its mouth. Totally predatory. "No, to having my baby."

"I'll get a menu." She turned and headed into the kitchen. Clover was losing the battle. More than anything, she wanted to hate him, but she was too busy relishing the kiss and picturing him naked.

Chapter Twelve

Nash couldn't deny it. The more he got to know Clover, the more he knew this was a perfect idea. She was beautiful, business savvy, and funny. So she was a bit of a hippie chick and loved the beach. In some ways, he could see how she would be good for him.

He couldn't remember the last time he had left the office early. Did a dentist appointment count?

I somehow doubt it.

Staring across the table from her, he hadn't brought up the question. She was avoiding it, but he wanted an answer. He shoved a piece of chicken around on his plate with his chopsticks and glanced at her. "Are you going to answer my question?"

She placed her chopsticks down and nodded. "Yeah, I debated the idea for a few fleeting seconds when I left your office."

He nodded. Clover suddenly had closed herself off and thrown him a wall. Why was that? "Can I ask why?" He knew if he prodded too hard, she would push away from him and not speak.

She slowly nodded and stared at the soda can on the table. She reached for it, but instead of lifting it, twirled it. "My father thinks I waste my time. I don't do nine-to-five. I take consulting jobs to surf and spend more time at the beach. Growing up, I had to be this perfect child, the ideal daughter, and the successful businesswoman. The beach was my retreat, and I quickly learned that surfing was the ideal adrenaline rush. Water, beach, no expectations, or my father in sight."

Nash shook his head. "Right, our fathers are friends. I should've known they would be similar in that way."

"Right." She rested her gaze on him. "I had no intentions of marrying and having a baby. That would be a good thing, even respectable and perfect." She appeared hesitant.

"I think this whole crazy threat of my father is insane. To top it off, he's threatening to sell the company if sales don't improve."

Clover nodded slowly. "I have a proven track record of increasing sales."

"Just before they merge or are sold?" He sounded a lot bitter and hadn't meant to be so terse.

"It doesn't have to work that way, " she assured, gaze locked with his.

"Clover, I had no intentions of getting married either."

Sadness etched itself into her pretty features. "I have the life I like, Nash. I won't be able to surf once I get married and have children."

He sighed and felt like they were just going in circles. "Can you save the company by increasing sales?"

Clover sighed. "You know by my resume I can."

"If you help me out, Clover, I'll give you as much say in the company as you want."

Pulling her bottom lip between her teeth, he knew she was thinking hard. "What if I agree?"

"That's up to you. We could go the clinic route. However, I think the old-fashioned way would be better."

"And I would get a complete say in the company, and you would *not* be bent out of shape—and alpha licking his wounds in the corner?"

"So you think I'm an alpha?"

"I think I have no clue what to do with you."

Nash grinned. Clover was cute when she wasn't so sure of herself. He leaned across the table and lowered his voice to a low, seductive tone. "Sweetheart, if you need ideas on what to do with me, I can help," he told her with a wink.

Her breath caught. "Why don't we start with calling a clinic?"

Nash lifted his brows, stunned at her words. "Is this a yes?"

"No!" She blanched. "But it's a very real *maybe*."

Not what he was going for, but it was a start. Then why was he disappointed and secretly wishing for more?

Chapter Thirteen

Clover was nervous as hell. She and Nash had fun yesterday afternoon, talking and remembering the summer when she was sixteen. When he had left, the kiss was short. She wasn't sure if she could kiss him again and keep her calm.

Too many more kisses like in Nash's office or in her living room would have her naked on the floor and sex happening. There could be worse fates, right? How bad could it be? Of course, with her luck, she would get pregnant, and there would be no going back.

Oh yeah, and agreeing to this was so much better.

They had phoned the clinic yesterday, and now Clover sat in a pastel office in a chair next to Nash. The chairs were in front of a desk belonging to a fertility doctor she hadn't met yet. They had filled out the paperwork and now were waiting for the man that might change her life forever.

This was bad. Clover should leave.

Too bad Nash had driven her vehicle home last night and to the appointment where they now were. The keys were in his pocket, leaving her trapped.

Her palms started sweating, and she ran them over her skirt-covered lap.

I want to leave.

"Don't be nervous," he assured her in a quiet tone.

She looked at him. "Nash, we're sitting in a fertility clinic." She blinked. "I don't even know your middle name."

"James." He smiled. "My middle name is James."

A whimper filled the room, and she frowned, realizing the pathetic sound had left her. It was as traumatizing as it was embarrassing. Nash's large hand reached over and covered one of her hands.

She swallowed and stared into the dark depths of his eyes. "We should go. This was a really, really—did I stress the fact this was a *horrible* idea?"

Nash nodded. "Relax, just breathe. It'll be okay." There was something sweet in his voice. "Just breathe."

She nodded, and her lips twitched, turning into a smile. Nash was actually being quite sweet.

This was still a really, really, really bad idea.

The door behind them opened, and footsteps entered the room.

I'm doomed—it's too late. Oh my God! I'm a coward! No! I'm in a fertility clinic with a man I never even dated.

"Ah, Mr. and Mrs. O'Leary." A graying man with a bit of a tummy and wire-rimmed glasses greeted them. He sat behind the desk. "I am Dr. Hamilton."

"Actually, we aren't married," Nash clarified, then cleared his throat.

"Oh!" The doctor forced a smile. "Why fix what isn't broken? Of course, more and more couples keep their names, share the bills, and a child, but never get married."

Oh, dear! Now he is a counselor?

Dr, Hamilton cleared his throat. "So, how long have you been trying to conceive as a couple?"

Oh hell!

She pulled her attention off the doctor to Nash, who blinked at her and exchanged a confused look. They both looked back at the doctor. Clover cleared her throat. "Um, not as long as you would think."

That was a good answer, right?

"Well, it's never too early to get checked. We are here to speed things along and help."

"Wonderful, right, sweetheart?" Nash asked and caused her to look at him.

"Fantastic."

What the hell else was she supposed to say? She focused on the doctor again.

"Today, we're just going to answer some questions, get a sample and check...." He glanced at the file. "Clover out." He again lifted his attention onto them.

Nash cleared his throat. "I can guess it's the wild man's army you want a sample of. Um, what exactly do you mean by checking Clover out?"

The doctor smiled. "Well, I have to do an internal on your wife." He paused. "You don't mind the term wife, do you? Or do you prefer something like a life partner?"

Oh dear, these questions are getting hard already.

Nash fidgeted in his seat. "Any is fine." His voice strained. She stole a glance at him. He started to appear unnerved.

Oh hell!

"Can we move to the questions?" Nash asked.

Something in his tone caused Clover to look at him. He was sitting rigid, and he had a crinkle on his forehead. His brows were furrowed, and his expression was far from happy.

Her stomach had a rock sitting in it, she was sure. She focused back on the doctor. He looked at her and smiled. "Clover, let's start with you."

"No!—No problem." She tilted her head and forced a light laugh. She should never have agreed to this. What if Nash wasn't a morning person or didn't like art? What if…?

"All right, Clover, are you on any birth control, or have you been in the last six months?"

Oh good, an easy question. "I've never been on it."

The doctor lowered the pen and started writing. "Good. How would you describe your menstruation?"

Nash leaned forward in his seat. "Is that really

an important question?" He rested his elbows on the desk. "I mean, isn't the whole objective here to stop her period?"

Oh my God! For being a player, he has absolutely no clue about women.

The doctor chuckled. "Now, Mr. O'Leary, it's all part of the routine. I just need to know if your wife is regular."

Nash's tanned skin turned ashen.

"Yes," Clover answered, hoping that would ease his tension.

"Wonderful, and the last date of that?"

Another easy question.

"Um, the 14th of February."

"Good, well, not good with it being Valentine's Day." The doctor wrote notes. He turned to Nash. "How often would you say you have sex weekly?"

Nash leaned back in his chair and said nothing. "Honey?" Nash finally glanced at her, and his eyes widened. He had no answer.

"I see." The doctor bounced his attention. "All right, when was the last time you had intercourse?"

It is hot in here. They should turn down the heat.

"I'm not sure," Clover muttered.

"Okay, Clover, I have a couple questions for you. Do you wish Nashville to stay?"

She sighed. It didn't matter at this point. "Nash can stay."

Hesitation worked over the doctor's face. "Some of these are very personal, are you sure?"

“I’m here planning parenthood. I think this should be okay.” She wanted to run from the room and building as if it were on fire and her life depended on it.

“Wonderful, an open relationship. Very well, how old were you when you became sexually active?”

“Oh, I haven’t.”

He smiled and nodded. There was movement beside Clover, and she could feel Nash’s intent stare.

The doctor cleared his throat. He reached for the bottled water on his desk and unscrewed the cap. “I meant when was the first time you had sex?”

Oh dear, the big question. “Technically, I haven’t.”

Chuckling, Nash shook his head beside her. “Clover! That makes you sound like a virgin,” Nash stammered.

Clover turned and stared at Nash, then swallowed. “Well, Nash, that’s because I am.”

Chapter Fourteen

That was the last thing he'd expected to leave her mouth.

Apparently, the doctor too, since the mouthful of water he had taken sprayed across his desk. Nash was stunned and angry she hadn't told him, and for a virgin, where did she learn to kiss as hotly as she did?

"I think I should leave you with your wife," Dr. Hamilton spoke.

"We aren't married!" she snapped at the doctor. Her cheeks flushed, and she shook her head. "And this happens to be your office." Her voice was calmer. "I'm leaving." She rose to her feet and shook the doctor's hand. "Thank you so much for your time." Releasing the doctor's hand, she turned and hurried to the door.

Nash was barely to his feet when she slipped over the threshold. "Thanks, doctor. We'll be in touch."

"Mr. O'Leary," Dr. Hamilton called as Nash headed towards the door. "You might want to try conceiving a child the old-fashioned way."

Nash's brows went up.

He's got to be kidding.

"You are aware of the basics, right? I mean, is there a problem with you that maybe we need to —"

"No, everything works, but right now, I have to talk to Clover." Nash raced out the door and didn't see her. However, the elevator doors closed.

This was bad.

He ran over to the wall and pounded the button as if his mere existence depended on it. Another elevator door opened, and he stepped on and then hit the button down, praying no one else got on between here and the main level of the medical building.

He was in luck and reached the bottom without a stop along the way. When he stepped off, he glanced around. Where could she have gone? He rested his hands on his hips and scanned the area. There was no sign of Clover. Sighing, he thought maybe she was waiting for him in her SUV.

He walked to where her silver Lexus sat in the stall and saw the white note under the wiper. He reached for it and read it.

Nash,

I'll see you at the office later.

Clover

"Wonderful." No, it wasn't fantastic. Nash wasn't amused and begrudgingly opened the vehicle. He needed to talk to her, and now he was worried about her. Why hadn't she told him she was a virgin before now? What difference did it make, and why now was she considering all this?

Nash frowned as he headed to the office. It was strange that he was worried about her. He just couldn't figure her out. How did Clover manage to be a virgin with a body like that this long? And what the hell was up with those kisses?

His cock started to ache, and he wanted to beat his head against the steering wheel. What the hell was he going to do? He liked her, he was more than sexually attracted to her, and she was a virgin. His mind riveted back to his original thoughts before he entered his office.

Nash barely remembered Sally saying Clover wasn't in and sulked. His emotions were out of whack, and so many thoughts ran through his head that he had no clue where to begin.

He sat there and wondered what to do. Nash noticed Clover's resume sitting there and reached for it. He picked up his phone and started calling the companies on it. Sure enough, they all said the same thing—increased sales, highest profit growth. There was no stopping her.

Nash glanced to the clock—still no Clover.

He got up from his desk and was going to ask Sally if she had arrived yet and just failed to find his office when Julie walked in through his office door.

"What's going on, Nash?" the buxom blonde greeted, obviously pissed.

Not now!

"With what, Julie?" He wasn't in the mood for

this and silently wondered if Clover had jumped a plane back to Florida.

She smiled at him and stepped forward. "I saw that look in your eye yesterday when the ad executive was there."

Oh hell!

"Julie now isn't a good time." He stepped around her, and she blocked his path to the door.

"Not so fast." Her hand came up to his tie, and he inwardly groaned. "Don't you even miss me?"

"You're the one that ended us, remember?" Nash remembered their break-up a little too well.

"Yeah, but now that I'm single again," she purred as she slid her hands up his shoulders. "I'm not asking for a commitment."

Why wasn't his body reacting to her? "Julie, I think you better get back to work."

A mischievous sultry giggle escaped her heavily glossed lips. "Why don't you work me over?"

He reached for her arms and clasped them. He needed to find Clover. "Julie now isn't a good time."

"It's just sex, Nash!" Julie exclaimed.

"Nash!" Clover's voice called from the entrance of his office, where she stood at a dead halt. "Never mind. I was just going to talk to you about flavors. Apparently, you're busy." She glanced at Julie, then met his gaze. "I'll go down to the freezer myself."

"Clover!" His words were lost as he shoved Julie away. He headed toward the door.

"Nash! You aren't actually going after her now, are you? Aren't you forgetting something?"

Nash paused at the threshold and looked at Julie. He could have her, but she was going to pose a problem now that Clover was around. "You're absolutely right. I am forgetting something."

She smiled and started to sway toward him. "So shut your office door and give it to me."

Nash grinned. "No, I can do this with my office door open."

Her features looked confused. Nice ass, decent in bed, but—

"You're fired." He spun on his heel and headed down the hall toward the elevator.

Why did Clover have to walk in right then? More so, what did she want to talk about flavors of ice cream for?

He pushed the button as the most pressing question entered his mind. Why, again, was he chasing Clover?

Chapter Fifteen

"What the hell was I thinking?" Clover fumed as she headed to the basement of the office tower. She should have known that men like Nash, hell, *all* men for that matter, preferred the cheap, accessible piece of ass.

Julie hated her on sight.

Clover sneered as she stepped off the elevator. Was it because Nash had paid attention to Julie instead of her? It didn't matter. Julie currently had Nash's full attention.

She paused and glanced around. Clover was in a basement with no clue where the freezers were. She turned to the elevator doors as they closed. This was turning out to be a terrible day.

Glancing at the blue sign on the wall ahead of her, she discovered it was a map. Stalking closer to it, she studied it and tried to shove Nash out of her mind.

She noticed the freezers were to the left and down the hall and focused on her high heels clicking against the cement. Clover had left the clinic and snuck off for comfort food. Pizza was the answer to everything chocolate didn't cover, which wasn't a lot.

She wondered why she had even gone to the clinic with Nash. Because he was hot and had suggested it. What kind of reasoning was that? What happened to her common sense?

It disappeared when she realized Nash was a hunk built for sex. He dampened her thong with a look, smile, or the sound of his voice and made her want to mount him like he was her new favorite amusement park ride.

She groaned. No man had a right to have that much power. Clover noticed the heavy silver doors and pulled at the handle. Nothing—it didn't budge. Of course not, because next to it was a keypad like an alarm system. "It's ice cream, people, not gold." She slid in front of it and read the green writing. "Please enter a valid identification number." She thought. "What the hell? I don't have a number."

She went to bang her head against it when footsteps caused her head to turn. "It takes the last four digits of your social security number."

"Thanks," she all but snapped at the object of her temper.

Damn, he looks good today. I've only noticed that since he picked me up and about a dozen times since then.

She punched in the number and heard the latch give on the door. Clover pulled the door open and stepped inside. She ran her hand on the wall, found the light switch, then flicked it between her fingers, and the light came on.

"Clover!"

Her nipples hardened, and she blamed the chilly air rather than his voice. She knew the truth and was a liar to tell herself he didn't affect her. "Not now, Nash."

Clover stepped deeper into the freezer and looked around for the size of the door. She thought the room would be bigger. Her gaze met rows and rows of Lucky Ice Cream pints. There were shelves with other stuff, but the metal shelving with more ice cream than she ever imagined stared back at her.

Nash's footsteps halted in the freezer doorway; she struggled not to turn and look at him, trying instead to remember why she had come down here in the first place. "Clover, we need to talk."

Martin from sales complained that the flavors were not hip enough. She was focused—that was another lie. Clover wasn't focused on anything but Nash's steps walking into the freezer behind her.

"Are you going to ignore me?"

"That's my idea!" she snapped. Why did Nash have to affect her? The door shut. She spun around and glared at him. "Tell me we can get out of here!"

He set his jaw and studied her. "Damn, you're pretty when you're pissed."

"Shut up, Nash!" She stalked past him, purposely brushing him with her shoulder. Too bad he was a hunky wall. He chuckled as she tried the handle. It opened, and her shoulders eased from their tense state in relief. Not so relieved, however, that she didn't turn and glare at him. "At least I am not stuck in here with you."

The expression on his handsome face revealed his frustration. "If we were locked in here, you would be forced to talk to me."

"Don't count on it," she answered, not even pausing.

Nash flashed her a wide grin. "You know it's your eyes. The spark to them when you're mad makes you rather striking."

Her temper started to kick into overdrive. "I so want to hurt you."

The lights flickered. Clover glanced to the ceiling as an uneasiness started to settle over her.

A small, sincere smile dusted across his full lips. "Relax, the construction crew across the street most likely bumped something."

She scowled at him. "Reassuring thought." Clover wanted to hate him; however, she really liked Nash. "Unless you're here to talk about ice cream flavors, don't you have Julie to return to?"

He grinned, and her breath caught. "About Julie...." The lights flickered again.

"I don't want to hear it!" She stepped around him.

"Stop being so stubborn! Hear me out."

A whirring sound sent her nerves on full alert, and she glanced to the door—the direction where the sound had originated. The gentle hum of the freezer stopped.

Nash sighed heavily. "Clover, would you please stand still and hear me out."

"No! I don't want to listen to anything you have to say," she replied dryly.

"We really should talk," he told her in a firm tone.

She studied him, then shook her head. "I don't want to talk, and you can't make me."

The lights went out with a *click.*

Clover pivoted around as red lights came on, and a sound resembling something metal falling into place echoed around them. She stared at the door and raced over to it. A sick feeling rocked her stomach as she tried to push the heavy metal open.

Nothing happened.

Nash's sigh filled the cold room. "It's all electrical. It's a safety mechanism for the ice cream in case of a power outage."

Clover turned as a jumble of mixed emotions hit the pit of her stomach, similar to a boulder. "You mean we are locked in here?"

His gorgeous face cracked into a grin, and a sexy chuckle left him. "Sweetheart, that's what I'm saying, which means you have no choice but to hear me out."

Dread, frustration, and a feeling she wanted to ignore washed over her. "How on earth did I ever get this unlucky?"

"Maybe bad for you and the ice cream that will melt—providing the power is off longer than ten minutes since the heater will kick on, and then we have to wait for the electrical system to cycle and restore the systems. It's all computerized. The freezer will return to chilling, and the door will return to the unlocked position."

"Another safety mechanism," she finished for him as her nerves became more unsettled.

Nash nodded once. "In case someone was ever trapped."

No, no, no, this is hell!

Despite the chill against her bare legs, this was it, and she was looking at a scorching version of Satan in Armani. "How long is a cycle?"

His smile broadened. "Six hours. That would give us plenty of time to talk."

And make my resistance to you futile.

"Talk about what? Ice cream flavors, I hope." She crossed her arms in front of her chest.

He stepped closer to her and locked his dark gaze with hers. "Flavors and the little matter of your virginity."

"What about it?" She tilted her chin up, hoping it would make her look determined that the topic wasn't open for discussion.

He leaned close to her ear, and his hands softly captured her upper arms. Nash's breath caressed the skin at the nape of her neck. "About how I plan on taking it from you, of course."

Chapter Sixteen

Clover shivered beneath his hold. Nash wasn't sure if it was from the cold or if he affected her. She hadn't liked seeing him with Julie, and Nash hated to admit it but liked her reaction. He enjoyed that she was temperamental and, dare he say, jealous.

She tried to pull out of his touch, but he tightened his grip. "Nash!"

Her perfume tickled his nostrils, and his body ached. Nash wanted her, and if he didn't miss his guess, she wanted him just as bad. "I want you to have my baby, Clover," he whispered, making damn sure every syllable touched the soft skin of her neck and ear with warm breath.

She struggled, but he wasn't letting go. "Why don't you ask Julie?"

Oh yeah, she's jealous.

He gently placed a finger under her chin and tilted her head so he could meet her doe-like gaze. The red lights gave an interesting ambiance. "I fired Julie, so you'd have one less excuse about being with me."

She blinked. Long lashes fluttered, and she blinked a couple more times as uncertainty worked its way across her pretty face. "You didn't?"

He smiled. At least Clover wasn't hostile. "I did. I'm very serious. I want you, Clover." He released his hold and glanced at his watch. "If luck is with you, the lights will return in nine minutes. If it's with me, we're here six hours, and I can convince you to have my baby."

"This is far from lucid." She went to step around him, and he snagged her in his arms.

"No, this is me wanting you the old-fashioned way. Wasn't it you that suggested sweat-soaked sheets and a condom-free environment?"

"It was a statement, not an invitation." Though her tone carried a terseness, the emotion didn't measure up to the expression on her face.

He glanced at her lips; the urge to kiss her was overwhelming. Kiss her and so much more. She shivered again. "Are you cold, or are you that affected by me?"

Clover groaned in what he guessed to be frustration. "I'm so glad to see your ego is back!"

"And I'm glad to see you're avoiding another question."

She inhaled deeply, and her chest rose slightly, accentuating her full round flesh beneath her top. Her lips pouted, and Nash was a done man. He lifted his gaze back to hers and stared at straight desire.

His hold on her tightened, tugging her close to his body as her lashes closed. She was the most beautiful thing in the entire world. As his lips touched hers, he waited for her to struggle. Instead, her arms looped around his neck, and her full breasts rested against his chest. Her lips parted, and a sigh escaped her.

Nash slid his tongue over her bottom lip and then into her mouth. His body warmed, and she pulled herself closer to him. Her tongue met his as her fingers laced through the hair at his collar. He lowered his hands and caressed her firm ass through her skirt. She shifted forward, brushing against his cock, which was getting harder by the second.

He removed his mouth from Clover's and studied her a moment.

"What's wrong?" She sounded nervous and insecure.

He blinked. Technically, nothing was wrong; everything was right. Though he was hesitant to ask the question on his mind, he truly wanted to know the answer—providing Clover told him. "Why are you still a virgin?"

The desire was gone from her eyes in a blink of thick, full lashes, and she stepped backward out of his arms. She distanced herself not just by that step but an invisible wall slammed up between them. "It's stupid."

"No, it's not. Clover, you are one of the smartest women I've met, maybe *the* smartest. Tell me."

Clover wasn't talking, and Nash had made

more progress kissing her. She looked at him, and though doubt was etched into her pretty face, she nodded.

"Originally, I was saving it for someone special," she began with hesitation. "Then I was saving it for when I got married. Only, I never got around to finding someone I wanted to commit myself to for better or for worse, and I got set into my life."

She covered her face with her hands and exhaled a puff of breath. "Then I avoided having sex because I was a twenty-eight-year-old virgin." She glanced up at him. "I didn't want to lose it in the backseat of a car. Nor did I want to lose it on a golf course by the light of the moon and a vinyl flag with a number on it."

What could he say? Nash was stunned. "Yet, you actually considered having my baby?"

She nodded and sighed. "Yep." Clover shook her head as if she couldn't believe it herself. "Everyone is allowed a moment of insanity."

"Unreal," he breathed.

"Yep," she agreed, glancing away, then darted a look back at him. "How much longer?"

He could tell Clover was upset over the situation. "We still have a few minutes."

She dropped her gaze down to the cement and stared at the freezer floor. Nash glanced around the room. What was he going to do?

What do I want to do?

He studied Clover a moment, who was now

hugging herself. It was easy, and the answer was obvious. Nash slipped his suit coat off and stepped toward her. He draped it over her shoulders, and she blinked up at him.

"You're cold," he stated softly.

"No, I'm affected by you." She whispered the confession, but he heard it clearly. A metal rattle started and then thudded like a hammer was being taken to it. Clover startled and blinked up at him wide-eyed. "Is that the power coming on?"

"Nope." His watch had been wrong, or his timing was off. What else was new? Lately, that had been the story of his life. "That's the generator for the heater. We have six hours."

Another heavy sigh escaped her full lips. "Wonderful, lots of time to discuss Lucky Ice Cream flavors."

"And other things," he added with the tilt of his head and a small smile.

"Like my virginity?" Her brows went up, and skepticism stared back at him.

His grin broadened. "That and other things."

Clover furrowed her arched brows. "Like what?"

He couldn't resist the urge to chuckle and placed his hands on her shoulders. "Us, the baby issue, which I will convince you of yet, and...."

She narrowed her gaze. "And what?"

Nash couldn't control his lips from turning into a grin. "You marrying me."

As Clover stepped out of his reach, she

blinked at him. “No way in hell!” She shook her head and stared at him as if he were a mad man. “You’ve lost your ever-loving mind, Nashville O’Leary. The answer is no. I mean a massive no way in hell.”

“Sweetheart, you’re trapped with me in a freezer, and I have a one-track mind. Consider this hell freezing over.”

Clover tilted her head up, focused on some imaginary spot, and finally lowered her gaze on him, wearing an unreadable expression. “You have six hours to convince me.”

Was she serious? “Really?”

She nodded. “I might be crazier than you, but yes, you have six hours. So I suggest you make them count.”

A strange sensation worked down Nash’s spine. He was happy, like genuinely happy. Without hesitation, he stepped toward her. “If you let me kiss you again, I can do it in six minutes.”

Her hand came to his chest, and she stopped him, keeping him at arm’s length. “I’m not going to make it that easy on you.”

“Sweetheart, I love a challenge.” And it was then he knew he was falling for her.

“Well, consider me your greatest one yet.”

She very well could be his greatest challenge. However, she was now officially his biggest turn-on, which was good.

Nash was falling for her and falling fast.

Chapter Seventeen

"They're where?" Charlie O'Leary yelled at Sally through his cell phone from the fifteenth hole. Mickey glanced from the putting green and cast him a puzzled expression. Charlie shook his head in disbelief. "You mean to tell me Nash and Clover are stuck in the freezer?"

His friend straightened and walked over to where Charlie was standing. "My daughter is where?"

He slid the cell phone from his mouth. "With Nash in the Ice Cream freezer."

Concern marred the other man's face. "Are they okay?"

"Oh yeah, the heat would have kicked on by now," he assured with a wave of his hand.

"Mr. O'Leary, they are locked in there for six hours. There is no overriding the system." There was a pause. "Are you there, Mr. O'Leary?"

He lifted the phone back up. "Yes, I'm here, Sally." He cleared his throat. "So there is no way out?"

"No, from what the alarm specialist says. The heat has kicked on, but they still have another five hours and fifty minutes. The heaters are going to make it warm. The ice cream will melt."

Charlie started to laugh. "And so will those two kids."

"Oh no, sir! It's not that hot," Sally assured.

Charlie laughed again and took in Mickey's grin. "Well, I better go, Sally. You say hi to the kids for me—whenever they get out."

Sally cleared her throat, obviously unhappy with how the conversation was going. Thankfully, she was a loyal employee and a professional ass-kisser. She wouldn't defy him. "Do you want me to see if I can get them out sooner?"

"No! Absolutely not. We wouldn't want to incur any unnecessary bills." He couldn't care less about cost; however, he did want his and Mickey's plan to run perfectly, and, though they hadn't counted on Nash and Clover's current situation, it certainly helped the project for a grandchild.

"But, sir, what if they get too hot?" Sally sounded panicked.

"That's what I am hoping for. Have a nice day, Sally." He ended the call. He grinned. "So my boy and your daughter are in a freezer that will do nothing but get warmer."

"You are a bad man, Charlie," Mickey laughed.

"Yeah, but so are you. It was your idea to offer Clover the job."

Mickey waved him off. "So, you think we'll get a grandchild?"

"We can hope." Charlie laughed.

Mickey sighed heavily. “I hope he marries her.”

Charlie patted his back. “My Nash is a good boy. He’ll ask. Of course, they’ll get married, and we will have those grandchildren.”

“It’s not your Nash I’m worried about,” his friend confessed hesitantly. “It’s Clover. She has no intention of getting married. Ever.”

“Do I sense a bet coming on? My boy is convincing when he wants to be,” Charlie exclaimed in delight.

Mickey sighed. “Yes, another bet, because Clover is as stubborn as they get. Makes my mother look like a saint.” He nodded and glanced at the fifteenth hole before looking back at Charlie. “Yeah, I bet you two dollars that she says no.”

“I’ll take that bet. Nash will be wedding and bedding her. You mark my words!” Charlie was more than confident.

Mickey shook his head and outstretched his hand. “This is one bet I hope you win.”

Charlie chuckled. “I will. Two whole dollars, huh? That was a lot of money back in our day.” He grinned, opened his cell phone, and punched a number. “Hey, Martin, this is Mr. O’Leary. Listen, are you alone?”

“No, sir, Sally and the maintenance guy are right here.”

Absolutely perfect. “Good, put the maintenance guy on.”

There was a shuffle and murmurs. “Hello?” A strange young voice greeted.

Mickey laughed, and his brown gaze sparkled. "You're a mean player," he accused.

"Yes, who am I speaking with?" Charlie asked the young man at the other end of the phone.

"Drew, my name is Drew, sir."

"Well, Drew, I need you to do me a little favor." He chuckled, debated, and knew that though this was evil, it would pay off in the long run.

"Of course, Mr. O'Leary, anything you want."

Charlie winked at Mickey. "Wonderful. Can you turn up the heat?"

Chapter Eighteen

"You know, for being Irish, I have bad luck," Clover told Nash and stepped away from him.

"Actually, I was thinking this is good luck. I have time alone with you, and no one can interrupt."

"You have a cell phone," she told him and turned around. "You could try calling someone to rescue us."

"Rescue you!" He placed his hand in his suit pockets and smiled. "I'm trapped in a room with a beautiful woman. Frankly, we could be here for ten hours."

Clover made a throaty growl sound, which was more cute than menacing. "And they call me stubborn."

"Actually, I find your determination a turn-on," Nash confessed. "My cell phone is in my inside pocket. Look for yourself. But there is no service."

I thought he was Satan, but now I realize he's a wolf, and I'm the lamb and his next meal.

She reached into his expensive suit coat pocket and pulled out the phone. Clover glanced at the face, slid the screen, and punched numbers.

"Who are you calling?"

"Your father to tell him what a scoundrel his son is."

Nash laughed, and the sound heated her body as it entered her ears and traveled over her spine.

The beeping sound was not a good sign. She removed the phone from her ear and studied the phone like it was the most treacherous thing she had ever seen.

Currently, it was.

She glanced up at Nash, who tapped a knuckle against the metal shelving. "Too much metal, a basement, and no reception. I should tell you I told you so."

He is so cocky. He's also sexier than hell.

"Of course, I won't gloat that I'm right because it will just make you mad, which will turn me on, and, frankly, I don't think my libido could take it right now."

She rolled her eyes and passed him back his phone. He was a scoundrel—a sexy, well-built scoundrel who wanted to marry and get her pregnant.

What the hell am I going to do?

She looked at Nash and debated a moment. Her surfing life would end, but so would her father telling her she wasn't amounting to anything. She would be married and would have a child. At one time, that was all she wanted.

When had that changed?

Nash frowned. "What's wrong?" He sounded

concerned. She wanted to scream and tell him to stop being friendly and likable.

It was right at that second she realized her worst fear. She had already started to fall for Nash. To make matters worse, she was considering his stupid plan more by the minute.

Nash closed the distance between them. "Clover, what's wrong?"

There's that concern again.

"Nothing is wrong."

Nash shook his head, and his dark eyes widened. "I don't believe you."

Oh my God! A gorgeous rich man wants me to mother his child and marry him.

She stepped backward.

I like him, I am sexually attracted to him, and he seems sincere.

"Clover, sweetheart, you are starting to worry me here." He glanced around and tugged at his tie.

Her temperature shot up as she watched his chest move beneath his crisp dress shirt. He yanked off his tie and undid the top buttons of his shirt. Oh yeah, it was definitely getting warm. His dark gaze didn't leave her. "Clover?"

She struggled to find her voice. "Would it be an open marriage?"

His dark brows furrowed. "As in dating other people?"

She nodded.

"No." He glanced away and shoved his hand through his hair. He looked back at her. "Let me guess, you are standing there wondering if I can be faithful?"

She nodded again, so afraid that if she moved the slightest bit, she would go over to him and give him her virginity, the moon, and a cheeseburger to go if he wanted.

She smiled. "If you had asked me on Monday, I would have said no way in hell."

"Well, a good thing for me that it's Wednesday and, as I recall, you are still saying no way in hell, but be warned, I can probably be just as stubborn as you."

The man had a good point. She tilted her head to one side. "True."

He chuckled and stepped closer. "When I'm in a monogamous relationship, I don't cheat." He paused and studied her a moment. "I think it would be effortless to be faithful to you."

Nash took another step. Clover's heart started racing, and she could no longer see her breath in the room. The heat was on, but she had an odd feeling that it wasn't just the heaters at play here. The sexual tension was thick and wrapped around them like a silk sheet.

His intense dark gaze remained steady on her. "You're actually considering this, aren't you?"

Just be honest.

"I actually am." Something caught Nash's attention, and he just walked away.

So much for that idea.

She turned to see him enter a small alcove

from where they were standing. He came back over with a blue quilted blanket. In a fluid swoop, he covered the ground. She then realized he had two of the heavy blankets. They reminded her of the ones movers had to protect furniture.

"It's going to be a while." He placed it on the ground and motioned for her to sit. "You might as well get comfortable."

She sighed, kicked off her high heels, and stepped over to the quilt. Nash raked his gaze over her, starting at her polished toenails up her legs, then laughed. "What's so funny?"

He met her gaze as she lowered to the blanket to have a seat. Might as well. They weren't going anywhere.

"Again, no nylons."

"I told you no. I'm not a bank robber."

"I don't care. You have great toned, tanned legs." He walked off, returned with two plastic spoons in clear wrap, and sat on the blanket next to her. "Just in case you decide you want ice cream."

She sat there as he grabbed the other quilt, put it behind him, and leaned against the shelf. He stretched his long legs out in front of him.

She took in the expensive fabric of his suit pants and glanced at him. "Do you always wear suits to work?"

"Yes."

She frowned slightly. "What about casual Fridays?"

Nash shrugged. "I never implemented them. Are you warm enough?"

Again, concern. It would almost be annoying if it wasn't so damn sweet.

"Would you?"

He smiled. "Are we negotiating?"

Nope!

"Maybe." She thought for a moment. "Yes."

"Yeah, I would consider having a casual day at least once a week. But no leggy cut-offs. Not here, and it's not that I don't appreciate them. I just don't need the guys in the mail room checking you out."

She laughed. Nash's tone and the situation were funny. "You sound so serious."

He shook his head. "I'd like it as much as you did when I was with Julie."

Oh yeah, that.

"I was a little put-out," she admitted quietly. "Thing was, I had no real reason to be."

"At least one you'd admit to yourself," he offered with a devilish grin.

"Well, there is that," she giggled.

His expression turned serious again. "Yeah, if the guys came onto you, I wouldn't be happy. So, if casual Fridays make you happy and promise you won't wear cut-offs, then yes. Next."

He was serious. Nash was serious about it all. Okay, surf's up. What did she have to lose? "Yes?"

"Yes, it's a yes." He groaned. "Now I'm talking like you."

She grinned, and the temperature shot up

at least another ten degrees. However, Clover doubted it had anything to do with the freezer's safety mechanism and everything to do with the chemistry between the two of them.

She shrugged off his coat and got to her knees. She inched her way closer to him and inhaled deep. There was no going back. She lifted a leg and straddled his hips. Nash's eyes darkened with desire.

"Yes," she whispered. She briefly grazed her lips against his.

"Clover..."

"Nash!" she teased and kissed his lips again.

"Do you have any idea what you are doing to me?" His voice was low, sexy, and so seductive. Her thong dampened, and she sat down against his groin. His cock was rock hard beneath her, and her pussy twitched.

"I notice I have your attention."

Desire blinked at her. "Clover, you need to get off me, or you'll have more than my attention."

She couldn't fight the smile that curved across her lips. Clover leaned in close to his ear and made damn sure her breath teased his skin as he had done to her. She was a virgin, not naïve. "Maybe, Nash, I want more than your attention."

His hands slid up and grasped her hips firmly. "Careful, Clover, I can only be a gentleman for so long."

"Yes, I'll marry you," she whispered.

She lifted her head and met his lust-filled

gaze, knowing she was a goner. Clover reached for his collar and lowered her face to his. Nash's mouth welcomed her with a carnal intensity that nearly sucked the air from her lungs.

Nash's tongue slid between her lips, and she couldn't resist the soft moan as the kiss deepened and ignited every nerve in her body. His hands came up from her hips and cupped her face.

He gently eased her head back from his. Their faces still were only inches apart. "I thought you didn't want to lose your virginity in the back of a car?"

She grinned and darted a quick look around. "Does this look like a car? If it does, we have bigger problems than the one I'm sitting on."

He grinned and lowered her head back to his. His hands left her face and slid to her back as he shifted her weight easily. Nash slipped Clover off his lap and eased her back against the quilted blanket, which, she was relieved, had looked clean, if anything. He lifted his head from hers, and her eyes opened. Nash stared down at her and studied her face a moment. "Are you sure?"

Despite being nervous and terrified, she was about to give him the worst sex of his playboy life, sure. "Yeah," she finally breathed, just a notch above a whisper.

He smiled wickedly, which jump-started her heart that was already racing a mile a minute. Nash brought his mouth against hers again, and her eyes closed. His hands roamed over her body, sending invisible flames over her skin, still covered by her clothes. She untucked his dress shirt and touched his bare skin.

Nash flinched slightly, then melted against her hands as they traced over solidly defined stomach muscles. He groaned against her tongue as his hand cupped a breast. Her nipples hardened and ached against the lace of her bra.

Clover arched her back to his gentle playing of her sensitive peak while his other hand teased along the skin of her leg. Her body shivered when his finger grazed against the soft material of her thong. He let out another groan and lifted his lips from hers. “You are so wet.”

She was beyond nervous, and yet... “I want you.”

“I can tell,” he whispered as if in awe.

The hand on her breast slipped off, only to work up under her skirt. Nash looped his fingers against the sides of her thong and tugged it off. After tossing the barely-there fabric to the side, he ran his hands over her legs and hiked up her skirt, revealing her naked lower half.

“Next time, we will be on a soft bed in a climate-controlled room.”

She smiled, trying to relax. “Yours or mine?”

He grinned. “Mine’s closer,” he replied, then dipped his face between her legs.

Her sudden embarrassment about being exposed vanished as his hot tongue slid across her folds and over her clit. His fingers toyed where his mouth had just been. She moaned and reached for his shoulders.

A large finger slipped inside her as his tongue teased and caressed the most sensitive spot on her body. Clover closed her eyes as the pressure built across her stomach. She caved to the erotic sensations heating her body from the inside out. Nash's lips, tongue, and touch movement picked up speed.

Clover thrust her hips against Nash's face as his tongue slid inside her and started working in and out of her pussy, then over her clit only to plunge back in a while his finger continued its rhythmic violation.

"Oh, God!" she moaned as the pressure broke and a wail of pleasure left her lips. His mouth clamped down, and Nash sucked. His tongue laved as her shoulders shook and the wave of pleasure rippled down her body.

Her breath was short, and she swore she would never take air into her lungs again. She finally forced out the little bit in her and struggled to inhale. Never had Clover experienced anything as intense.

Nash lifted his head and met her gaze. "Relax, sweetheart, we have a lot of time. I am just getting started."

Chapter Nineteen

Nash adored Clover and never in a million years could have predicted this. When she stormed away from him because of Julie, he was sure he had lost her, not only as an employee but also from Nash's life. Now he had her—the woman was actually going to marry him and, with some Irish luck, have his baby.

She sat up slightly and ran her hand over the front of his pants. His cock responded to her and continued to ache for release.

"I want you," she whispered softly through light, ragged breaths.

His gaze scanned her face. The last thing in the world Nash wanted was to hurt her. This was far from ideal circumstances, but there was no denying he wanted her too. He had wanted her from the moment she stepped into the boardroom. Her fingers slid to his belt and undid the zipper of his pants.

"Clover..."

She tilted her chin slightly and cupped her head as he lowered his mouth to hers. Her fingers played at the fabric, pulling his boxers and pants down with a tug. He braced himself for the cold air to touch his now bare flesh, but it didn't; the room was definitely warming up. Her hand wrapped around him, and she looked up at him.

Control was something he had always prided himself on. However, watching Clover climax and having her taste on his tongue had almost done him in. With lust in her eyes and her soft hand stroking his cock, he was just about at the brink of his control. "God, you're sexy," he whispered.

She simply smiled, and he gently removed her hand from him and eased her back. His hands caressed her as he covered her body with his and slowly moved up her. His cock teased against her satiny soft skin and then grazed over the wet folds of her pussy. She was completely smooth, no doubt from her swimwear time.

He eased his tongue across her parted mouth, and her body relaxed as he planted warm, wet kisses over her neck. Her collarbone was defined as he slid his tongue over the soft skin. She moaned quietly, and he shifted his body between her toned, tanned legs, which separated, granting him willing access.

The tip of his dick played at her entrance, and his mouth claimed hers as he entered her. The faint resistance broke, and she whimpered. Nash stilled his movements, giving her time to adjust to the new sensation.

Realization hit him full force as he was buried deep inside her tight, wet pussy—he was the first man to ever have the beauty beneath him. Nash lifted his mouth from hers and glanced down at her. Her eyes opened, and he stared into her dark eyes. "Are you okay?"

Clover's gaze caressed his face and her lips, puffy from their kiss, turned at the corners in a smile between sweet and sexy. "Fine. Please, don't stop."

"So stubborn!" he whispered as he gently moved inside her wet cavern, which hugged his cock tightly. He wasn't sure how long he would last, but more than anything, he wanted her to enjoy this.

Clover slipped her arms around his neck and tugged him into a carnal kiss, further fueling his desire. Nash slid his tongue into her mouth and met Clover's as he slowly started working his cock in and out of her.

More than anything, he wanted to bring her to climax again before he exploded inside her, and Nash had little doubt he would be cumming hard and fast soon. He was surprised when she wiggled beneath him, pulling him deeper into her. She was so wet and tight. He groaned against her tongue and increased the speed of his thrusts.

He always wore condoms, except for now.

The sensation was incredible as she started to rock her hips into his thrusts. He quickened his pace, wanting to reach deeper inside of her. Her legs spread further apart, granting him further access. He knew he wouldn't be able to last much longer when her lips pulled from his.

Clover's back arched, and her head tilted back. She moaned loudly, and her puffy, overly-kissed lips looked unbelievable as he opened his eyes. Pleasure washed over her pretty features. Her pussy walls tightened around him with such a force his resolve broke, and he plunged into her with a powerful thrust.

"Oh fuck!" he growled as he emptied his release into her.

"Oh God!" she gasped as he struggled for breath. Beneath him, her body stiffened, then trembled. Her pussy pulsed in convulsions before again milking his cock in a hard grasp as she climaxed again.

He couldn't believe how intense his orgasm had been or how she had given herself to him without hesitation. Next time, he would ensure they were on a soft bed or in the hot tub at his penthouse.

Her breath was as ragged as his. He should have stripped her naked, but urgency had won out. She glanced at him through thick lashes, and his heart slammed to a stop. Clover was stunning, and he was already short of breath—the expression on her face wasn't helping.

"Was that okay?" she asked softly, so quietly he had almost missed the question altogether.

Holy hell? Did she doubt?

He smiled at the woman who he was still buried balls deep in. "Sweetheart, it was more than okay."

She smiled. "Oh yeah," she answered with a breathy giggle.

Oh yeah was right.

He lightly brushed her lips with his. Maybe this marriage thing wasn't going to be so bad after all.

Chapter Twenty

Now that they were presentable again, and Clover had her panties on again, she had to admit she felt good about her decision. It was weird since she had apprehensions about moving out to LA. She didn't miss Florida as much as she thought she would.

If anyone had told her a week ago that she would end up in a hot freezer with a hotter man, she never would have believed them. Especially if they told her she would lose her virginity, agree to marry a gorgeous guy, consider having his baby, and then sit eating half-melted ice cream with the hunk she had decided to be a wife to.

"So, do you think I should tell our dads about our latest development?" Nash stared at the white plastic spoon he had just pulled out of his mouth and then dipped it back into the chocolate mint ice cream.

"Good question." She stood and glanced around the shelves. "Do we carry pistachio?"

"Nope. Do you want me to?" he asked in seriousness.

She glanced at him and flashed him a wide

grin. "God, you're easy."

He chuckled. "But only for you, sweetheart."

She rolled her eyes and turned, scouting the flavors on the shelves.

What would I tell my parents? Should they know, or would they think this was another flighty move on my part?

Clover's father had pressured her to do this for Charlie, who had practically done everything but get down on his knees and beg. She stopped and looked back at Nash. "Nash, when did you know I was coming for the job? I think you said that you had found out just that morning."

"About twenty minutes before you dragged your sand-covered feet and long, tanned legs through the door." He took a spoon full of ice cream and frowned. "When did you know you were taking the position?"

"Long enough to fly out and get an apartment, have my SUV and furniture delivered, work on my tan, and—three weeks."

"You knew for three weeks?" A questioning expression marred his face, and she wasn't fond of the look.

Her brows furrowed, and insecurity started tensing the muscles in her shoulders and back. "What are you thinking?"

Oh God, he's thinking. Not good.

He blinked yet kept his gaze fixed on her. "My dad approached you for the job?"

"Yeah, and I said no at first." She spotted a row

of fudge ripple and leaned down to grab one of the containers.

Why wouldn't he tell Nash I was coming?

She reached for one of the quarts when the answer hit her. Realization struck as she straightened, and the ice cream slipped out of her hand.

Nash jumped up and was at her side in record time. "What's wrong? I didn't hurt you, did I?"

She glanced at him as a hard ball resembling a rock formed in the pit of her stomach. "I'm an idiot."

He frowned. "No. Remember what I said about the smartest woman I've met." He glanced at the partially melted ice cream on the floor. "There are rags over in the alcove." He glanced back at her.

"Your father…my dad…oh my God, Nash. We played right into it." She was positive her expression matched the mixed emotions flooding her.

I'm going to kill my father.

Nash's back stiffened, and he narrowed his gaze on her. "You think they set us up?"

She nodded. "That would be my best guess, yes."

Nash shook his head. "Knowing the pair, they probably bet on us, too."

She winced and looked away. "That sounds like them." Clover turned and went to step around him. There were so many thoughts and emotions running through her. She had no clue where to even begin to figure things out. She had been played by her dad and fell into Nash's arms hook, line, and sinker.

And he fell into parts of my body no man had gone before. I'm a stupid idiot.

Nash's strong hand caught her wrist, and she paused then glanced up at him. "Do you regret it?"

She smiled and shook her head. "No. I think we'll be okay. I just don't like being played."

He drew her closer to him and released her wrist so he could wrap his arms around her. "I won't hurt you, Clover."

She couldn't believe her dad and was ready to chew his ass out. Not that Nash wasn't a hunk and obviously more than taken with her. Still, her dad and Charlie were out of line. She placed her hand on his chest. "I know, but that still doesn't stop my wanting to phone my father and scream at him."

He grinned and lifted a brow. Sinful was an excellent word to describe Nash, and he leaned in and kissed her lips. "So, my dad and yours convinced you to come here, and then my dad dropped the bomb on me last minute with a crazy ultimatum." He closed his eyes. "They planned this and counted on us doing what we've done."

"Yeah." What could she say? He was right.

"Unreal, totally unreal." Nash released her and shoved his hands in his pockets as he started to pace the floor not covered by the quilt. He then stopped and met her gaze. His expression was solemn. "I'm sorry."

Oh, dear.

"For what?" She regretted the words as soon as they left her tongue.

"You being manipulated into this crazy scheme." He shoved a hand through his dark hair. "It's bad enough you're cleaning up the mess I made of this company. Now you are in the vortex of my father getting back at me and proving I'm nothing but a careless playboy."

Her stomach ached, and a weight settled over her chest. "I had sex with you and agreed to marry you because I wanted to, Nash. I need to settle down, according to my father."

She sighed as if the world's weight rested on her shoulders as Nash resumed his pacing. With the sudden tension tightening across her back, it felt like the entire globe rested at the base of her neck.

"Besides, I need to have more say in the company, and you need a baby, if not an ally if you want to stop the sale of this company." She sighed again. Her business sense kicked in, but so did her fears. Her stomach flipped, and her heart raced. "Are you upset?"

He stopped pacing and looked at her. "I have a beautiful, smart woman, willing to have my baby and marry me. No, I would say life is pretty good. I somehow can't imagine things getting boring with you."

Clover smiled, and some weight lifted off her, though it didn't ease the strain. She braved a step closer to him, and he stepped towards her, meeting her part way. “I’m glad you still want me.”

His brows shot up, and he enveloped her in his arms. “I want you. Hell, I could have you again right now if the truth is known. However, I’m waiting until we’re in more comfortable surroundings.”

He kissed her lips briefly, and the feel of his cock hardening through his pants caused her pussy walls to tighten. He lifted his lips, and she opened her eyes. “We can drive to Vegas on the weekend and get married.”

She nodded, and a thoughtful look crossed her face. “Nash, do you think we could maybe date after we get married?”

“I’d love that.” He paused, then chuckled. “We are doing this completely backward. You know that, right?”

“Thanks to both of our fathers, who nudged this along and threw in some peculiar conditions. I wonder who won the bet.”

Nash grinned. “I have no clue, but wouldn’t it be fun to play them at their own game for once?”

“You’re evil,” Clover giggled.

His gaze dropped to her lips, then met hers again with lust. “But you like it. I can tell by your smile.”

Any idea to get back at the two meddling and manipulating fathers she would take under serious consideration. “What’s your idea?”

He shook his head. “No way. First, this.”

Nash lowered his head towards hers, and their lips met. Heat ignited her body, and her pussy ached as she parted her lips, and his tongue thrust into her mouth. Wetness pooled between her legs again, and desire rippled through Clover at the discovery of his cock hardening. He groaned against her tongue, then lifted his mouth from hers, not before licking her lower lip.

"Now, will you tell me your idea for the fathers?"

He grinned. "Oh yeah, but for the record, you're staying at my place tonight."

She frowned slightly. "Why can't we stay at mine?"

Nash kept her in his arms. "Because mine is closer to the office, we can spend longer in bed."

"Excellent point," Clover laughed. She already didn't recognize her life in less than a couple hours. "So, what are you thinking?"

Chapter Twenty-One

Nash unlocked his penthouse door. He was glad to be out of the freezer. He was glad they had gone to Clover's to grab her suitcase. She came across as sad as she left her apartment and surf gear behind.

He had to admit she had a beautiful walk-up place on the beach. Nash also knew she would probably miss it being back in LA. He stepped over the threshold with her suitcase and flipped on the light. She slowly walked in behind him and paused.

He turned his attention to her as she looked out the large window to the lights of the city. She turned and smiled at him. "Nice view."

Setting the suitcase down, he turned and walked over to the door. He shut it behind Clover and smiled. "I thought you said I couldn't pay you to live in LA?"

Clover smiled faintly. "You're not. You're marrying me."

She had him there. He stepped toward her. "Why don't we hang out at your place on weekends?" He grinned. "Not this weekend since we're getting married, but after that. You can teach me how to surf."

She blinked and looked unconvinced. "Really?"

"Yeah, I spend enough time in a tanning bed. It'll be fun and do me some good to catch some real sun for a change." He sighed. "Our lives are becoming unrecognizable."

She nodded, and he felt terrible. "It's okay, Nash." Clover put her hand on his chest and smiled up at him. "We're out of the freezer and have a plan, so let's implement it."

He bent his head toward her and kissed her lips. "Can we shower first?"

She shook her head, indicating she didn't think it was a good idea. "No, because I'm pretty sure that ass-kiss Sally has already called your dad, who is either with my dad or has called him."

She had a good point. Nash's father hung out with Mighty Mickey a lot. If he had remembered how beautiful Mickey's daughter was, he would have flown out to see his parents, just to see Clover. "Sally, Martin, and even Fritz have been with Lucky Ice Cream for years. They're all very loyal to my dad." He grinned. "I'm so glad that someone else finds Sally a suck-up."

"Yeah, she's a problem, especially if we pull this off." Clover sighed. "You said that they were all loyal to your dad. Nash, get them to be loyal to you."

Defeat trickled down his spine, and his happy

mood faltered. "They think I'm a womanizing playboy."

Clover's laughter filled the room around them and improved his mood instantly. He liked the sound and was looking forward to hearing it often. "You *are* a womanizing playboy."

He grinned, grabbed her arm, and pulled her close to his body. "I *was*."

"Let's call the dads," she whispered, then stretched and softly kissed his lips.

Nash didn't want to admit it, but things had changed rapidly between them, and he wasn't minding it as much as he thought he would. "Okay, then you're completely mine."

She laughed and stepped away from his touch. "Such a spoiled brat."

"Such a stubborn beauty," he shot back as he walked over to the cordless phone and snagged it. He glanced at her, and Clover pulled her cell phone from her purse. She walked over to him, and the phone started to ring. He hit the speaker and wiggled his brows.

"Nash! Thank God you're home!" his father greeted over the house phone. He could tell that his father had him on speakerphone as well; Mickey was no doubt there.

"Hi, Dad."

"Are you and Clover all right?"

Nash set the phone down on the table and exchanged a look with his future wife. "Dad, how did you know I was with Clover?"

Clover mouthed *Sally* at the same time his father said the older secretary's name. "She was kind enough to phone and let me know that the construction crew knocked out the power, and you and Clover were trapped in the freezer."

Clover rolled her eyes. *Told you,* she mouthed.

Nash had figured, too. Here went nothing. "Dad, about Clover. She's not going to work out at the company. She quit."

He darted a glance to Clover. She bit back a giggle; she was beautiful and his. Tomorrow, she would be his wife, then they would date, and maybe eventually—

"What the hell do you mean she quit?"

Oh yeah, dear old dad is pissed. Time to drop another grenade.

"She said she refused to work in advertising. It was a long six hours." He winked at Clover. "I managed to convince her to stay. However, she isn't working in advertising. She is coming on as a consultant and working with me directly."

His father's chuckle echoed through the phone. "Are you sure you want to do that, son?"

"I have no choice. You threatened to sell the company if I didn't increase sales," Nash reminded his dad.

"I also told you that you had to get started on a grandchild for me," he chuckled.

Nash cocked an eyebrow as Clover scowled at the phone and met his gaze. She lifted her hands and pretended to strangle the air. Nash wanted to laugh. “Yeah, well, I’m trying.”

“You could always try with Clover Callaghan.”

“Well, you see, Dad, about that... I would really love to, but I can’t.”

“Why the hell not?” his father bellowed. Clover startled. He slipped an arm around her waist, kissing her cheek softly. He couldn’t believe he was about to do this.

“Well, Dad....” He tightened his hold on her, and Clover covered her mouth with her hand.

“Well, what? She’s beautiful, Nash, and my best friend’s daughter,” his father stated the obvious.

“I know that, Dad.” Nash’s gaze held Clover’s. “But she’s also marrying someone else.”

There was silence from the other end of the phone. Nash wanted to laugh.

“What on God’s green earth?” Mickey roared. Clover had guessed right, and the fathers were together. “What do you mean my daughter is marrying someone else?”

Chapter Twenty-Two

Clover struggled not to laugh as Nash said goodbye to his father and stepped around her to end the call. It was funny her father was having a fit. Her cell phone started to chime, and she answered it at the same time that Nash turned back to her. "Hi, Daddy, what's up?"

"Clover Callaghan, what the hell are you doing?" She held the phone away from her ear, and Nash leaned in, resting a hand on her hip. "I just found out from a friend that you are getting married! Your mother is going to be a wreck. How dare you not even tell your parents about this?"

Nash snickered.

She wanted to laugh. "It was all rather sudden," she explained as Nash released her hip and slipped off his suit coat. He tossed it over a chair. She smiled at the expensive tie hanging out of its pocket. He stood in front of her and placed both hands on her hips. Her father was barking about something, but she was far more interested in Nash.

She had no clue what her father had said, but since he had stopped, she figured she should say something. "Oh, Dad, I'll fly out in a few weeks, and you can meet him."

"I don't want you bringing some strange man to the house. Clover, this tops it out of all your crazy, flighty ideas."

She sighed. Typical of her father. Nash rolled his eyes; he didn't look impressed. Could it be that her father reminded him too much of his own? "Dad—"

"So help me, Clover," and he was off again on another tirade. She tuned him out.

Nash tugged and drew her closer to him. His lips found the sensitive part of her neck, and he planted warm kisses on the side opposite where she held the phone. Her body heated to his kisses and her nipples hardened. Clover's legs warmed, and she reached for his strong arm to steady herself.

She stepped out of her high heels. Her bare feet touched the soft, plush carpet beneath her. "Dad…."

Her dad continued to rattle on about irresponsibility and selfishness. Nash continued kissing her, and Clover's pussy pulsed as he started walking her backward down a hall. She let him, as her father kept chirping like a bird on the first day of spring. Clover was quite sure it was Charlie in the background complaining about Nash.

"Dad, enough!" she all but screamed into the phone.

Nash flipped on a light, and she glanced

around to discover she was in his bedroom. The room was decorated with expensive black furniture and was quite elegant. Nash's hands had already gotten her blouse untucked, and his hands roamed over the flat of her stomach.

God, he feels good.

She bit back a moan.

"Clover, are you even listening?" her father demanded.

She had no clue what her dad had said before that. She struggled to find her voice as Nash's hands slid up and under her blouse. "Nope, can't talk. Stomach. Bye." She hit the call end button and struggled to set it on a nearby dresser. Once accomplished, she laced her fingers through Nash's hair and played with the silky strands.

He lifted his head. "I have a different idea instead of a shower."

She blinked at him as he quickly undid her blouse, peeling it and her jacket off. Both articles of clothing fell to the floor. He leaned in and traced her collarbone with his tongue. She couldn't believe she'd waited this long to have sex. Her body wanted him again.

Who the hell was she kidding? She wanted him about ten minutes after he climaxed inside her in the freezer.

"What did you have in mind?"

Nash glanced at her, his dark eyes filled with heat and desire. He carefully turned her around to look out a large window. There, off the bedroom, was a door leading to the balcony and a large hot tub. She darted a look back at him in surprise. He slipped his hand in hers. “Come on.”

He led her through the door and grinned. She was amazed at the hot tub size; it looked like something you would find at a hotel. Stopping in her tracks, he released her hand and stepped back to kick off his shoes and remove his socks.

He pulled his shirt and then tossed it on a nearby deck chair. Under the soft glow of early evening, his perfectly defined chest and wonderfully chiseled abs rippled. Her breath caught as he closed the distance between them.

“You obviously hit the gym,” she whispered, sure all the salvia was gone from her throat and her voice.

He shook his head and reached to the back of her skirt. “No, I swim every morning in the lap pool downstairs.”

That would do it.

His fingers found the zipper and slid it down while his other hand cupped her ass. Both hands left her long enough for the skirt to fall. His eyes raked over her. “Tell me you own a lot more sets like that.” Referring to her soft cotton-stretch lace bra and thong.

“All my sets are pretty much like this,” she confessed.

“Perfect.” He snaked his arms around her, and she reached for the belt and zipper of his pants. His mouth came down hard on hers, and his tongue licked and played before thrusting in her mouth. Their tongues met. She touched the strong muscles of his stomach, then dipped below the soft fabric of his boxer shorts to his rock-hard cock.

Clover wrapped her fingers around the solid size. How it ever fit in her was still a surprise to her. His tongue continued to entwine with hers, and he groaned against her mouth.

He removed his lips from hers and his lashes opened. Clover smiled wickedly and stepped back. Unfastening her bra from the front, she allowed him a full view of her breasts. Nash slid his pants and boxers down as she discarded her bra and thong. Her pussy was sensitive from arousal.

Nash's strong leg muscles moved, and his erection stood bold as he stepped toward her. He was beautiful, a perfect specimen of the male form. He kissed her again. "Get in." He sounded primal and completely alpha. Her walls clenched in anticipation as his gorgeous body moved to a button.

The water was warm as she climbed in, nervousness fluttered in her stomach as the jets kicked on, and she sat back in the water. The night air seemed cool compared to the temperature of the water and the heat in Nash's eyes as he entered the hot tub. He fell to his knees and worked his way over to where she sat.

His lips curved into a grin. "This is so much better." He paused, and his eyes scanned her face.

Clover's heart picked up speed. "What?"

"I just can't believe this." His voice was a low whisper as his hand touched her legs as he talked. "Do you know that you turned me on the moment I saw you?"

She smiled. "No. I did wonder why you didn't stand."

He chuckled, and her skin flamed, her nipples hardening to the point they ached from the sound alone. "Why I didn't stand?" His hand covered hers, and he lifted it to his cock. "I was about this hard in twenty seconds flat, and it made things uncomfortable."

She giggled and wrapped her hand around him. His shoulders shifted slightly as her hand worked up and down on him. Nash lowered his head to capture her mouth, thrusting his tongue deep inside. His fingers worked up her legs to the sensitive spot between them.

Moaning against his tongue, Clover tightened her hold on his arousal. His fingers grazed over her clit as both hands moved to her hips. She released his cock, wrapping her arms around his neck. He lifted her slightly and repositioned himself; his tip teased her clit where his fingers had been.

Another moan left her as he pressed deep inside. It was what she needed, despite needing a moment to adjust.

Finally, she moved her hips slightly, and he worked in and out of her as Nash's tongue did the same to her mouth. The pressure increased across her belly, and she wanted more of him. She bucked her hips against him, and he picked up speed.

Nash groaned as she pulled her lips from his and her arms around his neck. She cupped his face in her hands and stared into his eyes. The pressure broke, and as her pussy walls clamped around him, she whimpered and held his face.

He thrust one final time, and pleasure poured over his handsome face. His cock throbbed inside Clover as he found his release and emptied it inside her.

Her breathing was ragged, her shoulders shook, and her entire body trembled as she climaxed again. Nash's breathing was short and husky as he looked at her and shook his head. "Incredible."

She nodded that it was.

He cast a crooked grin. "And it's only going to get better."

That was something a little beyond her comprehension. She knew, though, that if the sex was any indication, she and Nash would only get better.

Chapter Twenty-Three

Nash caught himself actually whistling twice the following day and once over lunch. He was in an incredible mood. It still nagged at him about how Mighty Mickey had gone off over Clover. However, he reminded himself that the man kept company with his father. He had left early for the office and let Clover sleep.

His lips curled into another smile as he thought of the night before. The sex was incomparable, and the way they talked with ease for half the night about what they had done and seen over the years seemed normal. Everything between them seemed normal like they had known and been together longer than they actually had. They had agreed to play it cool and not let anyone at the office know what was happening.

He had purposely avoided her but knew she had meetings with a few department heads.

Nash walked toward where their offices were and noticed her door open. He paused in the doorway and remained quiet. She was bent over work on her desk and shook her head disapprovingly.

Clover groaned and tossed down the pen in between her fingers. If he was going to marry her, she needed a ring. He smiled. No, she needed a rock, something that would have Sally reporting to his dad in record time.

She scowled at the document on her desk and glanced to the door. Her face broke into a perfect smile, and his heart raced. “Nash!”

He crossed the threshold and shut the door behind him in a single step. Nash glanced to the blinds on her office window, thankfully closed.

“I don’t think I told you how amazing you look today.” His attention fell to the stack of files that were scattered everywhere. “I know for a fact these weren’t here this morning.

She winced. “Nope, they arrived over lunch—oh my God! We were going to go to lunch.”

“I had to deal with things over the freezer and throwing out a lot of ice cream, so I haven’t gone yet. Sally told me you were in meetings with Martin and Fritz.” He surveyed the room again, then focused on Clover as she turned in her chair. Nash sat on the edge of the desk.

“You were gone when I woke up,” she told him quietly.

“My car was here, and I didn’t need Sally questioning things, so I came in early.”

She lifted her brows and stood. “Can I get a kiss now?”

“I can give you more than that,” he teased,

genuinely happy to be alone with the woman who had become a vice.

Her brows dipped as if she didn't like that idea. "Maybe later? But I'll take that kiss." She stepped closer to him, and he gently caught her in his arms.

"A little tender today?" He worried maybe they had overdone it last night in the hot tub, then again in the bed.

It might have been a bit much.

"I'll be okay," she assured and pressed her lips to his. His body ignited, and his hand slid up her back to the back of her head. He gently cupped it, allowing his tongue to slide across her lower lip. Her mouth parted, and he slipped his tongue inside. His body wanted her, but he didn't want to hurt her. Nash withdrew from the kiss, and her lashes fluttered open.

"That was worth the wait," she breathed in blatant honesty while her dark eyes sparkled.

He kept her in the wrap of his arms as he glanced around again at the files. Nash returned his gaze to her and lifted a brow. "What did you get yourself into?"

"Market reports," she replied, losing her smile. "The good, the bad, and the—"

"How ugly is ugly?"

Her lips pursed together. "Nash." She hung her head, and it was apparent she wasn't happy.

Nash sighed and released her. "Okay." He allowed Clover to step back and walk around, grabbed one of the chairs in front of her desk, and moved it next to her chair. "Let's sit, and you can tell me all about it."

She smiled faintly and reminded him of a little girl. He wondered if they would have a boy or a girl. A boy would be cool, but a little girl that looked like Clover would be okay, too. Maybe, one of each. No, that could be bad. There were too many guys like him out there.

No way, not a girl.

"Why are you frowning? I haven't told you the bad news yet," Clover asked with concern.

He chuckled. "I was just thinking...."

She tilted her chin down. "About what?"

Nash motioned her to sit, and she did so. He sat in the one he pulled up. How honest should he be? Nash was already thinking of more than one child and— "How if we had a girl, I'd be worried about guys like me."

Her brows shot up.

Laughing, he rethought that. "At least, what I was like." His smile faded. "I'm really starting to like us, Clover."

She hesitated and thinned her full lips. "I like us, too." She shot a glance to the files and looked back at him. "Nash, this could take a while to fix."

"I think we are going to be amazing together."

She smiled and shook her head. "I think we will be, too, but I was referring to increasing sales."

Nash frowned. That wasn't good. Actually, it was horrible news. "We don't have time."

"Well, we have a problem because it's not the

quality or the marketing. It's our competition."

He didn't like the way this conversation was going. "Just spit it out, sweetheart. We can figure it out, so what's the problem?"

She swallowed. "From what I can tell, it's most definitely the product. Nash, if you want to fix this, we better quickly develop some fun, interesting flavors and get exposure to it."

"Oh hell, you're saying we need a miracle."

She blinked and stared at the files. "I would go over this with you, but you're probably busy."

Nash blanched. "Actually, no, I have time. I have come to a horrible conclusion."

"Do I dare ask?"

He sighed and smiled. "I don't really do anything except make the final decision. I waste a lot of time doing nothing, and now that I'm not hitting on staff members, I have even more free time."

Clover's look narrowed, and her head tilted. "Well, since you're the boss, let me bring you up to speed." She lifted her hand to reach for a file.

Nash took it, and she glanced back at him. "Clover, if we have a child together, we're running this company together."

She smiled. "That sounds fair to me."

It was fair. What wasn't fair was that Nash was beyond doubt falling in love with her. Marriage and a baby, yes, but never had love come into the equation. Then again, Nash never knew he was capable of it or that someone as incredible as

Clover existed.

Chapter Twenty-Four

It was the company's first casual Friday, and Clover sat in the boardroom trying not to focus on how the currently pacing Nash looked in his fitted jeans and golf shirt. His strong arm muscles were exposed, and he was definitely gorgeous.

She liked the way they got along.

Despite their rocky start, which Nash confided to her in bed this morning, he was sure was pure sexual attraction. She liked him, and for a person who guarded her heart like she had her virginity, she was losing the battle.

Clover was falling in love with him. They talked for hours, laughed like friends, and respected each other professionally. How could she not?

The real Nash wasn't so much a playboy. He was actually quite intelligent. He did care about the company and, like her, had something to prove to his father.

He finally stopped. "No one can come up with an original flavor for ice cream." Stressed, he glanced at Martin, who was staring at his lunch. "Martin, what's wrong?"

"I'm hungry, sir."

Nash placed his hands on his hips, and his shirt stretched across his defined chest. "Then eat. Everyone can eat," he exclaimed and shot a frustrated look to Clover, who just smiled.

Neither of them had eaten since they were leaving early to drive to Vegas. The next day, they were getting married, and Monday, it was back to work and the charade. They were also going to leave about fifteen minutes apart; they were careful. They had to be. Especially since she was dodging her father's calls like she would a lousy date.

Nash started his pacing again, and she glanced around the room. Okay, next problem. How could they give it exposure fast if they were to come up with something?

"Who has peanut butter?" Clover asked.

Again Nash halted his caged animal routine and glanced at Clover, sniffing the air like a dog before a rain storm.

"I do," Martin answered as she stared across the table at him.

Her attention fell on the sandwich in Martin's hand. Yep, peanut butter on what appeared to be one hundred percent whole wheat. Clover went to turn away when something between the slices caught her eye.

She blinked, and her eyes widened. Without thinking, she hopped out of her chair and crawled across the table. "Nash?"

"Clover, what are you doing?" He asked, no doubt wondering what was running through her pretty head.

"Martin, is that banana on there?"Clover asked.

The other man looked around the sandwich at her. "Um, yes?"

"I loved peanut butter and banana sandwiches when I was a kid," one of the department heads noted.

"I still do," Fritz piped up.

"That's flavor number one." Clover climbed off the table and turned to Nash. He grinned and nodded. She was brilliant and going to be one hundred percent his—not that she was anything less now. He walked over to her and picked her up in his arms.

"Genius!" He went to kiss her and paused. They exchanged a horrified expression as both realized what they had just done and glanced at the table of stunned executives.

"Oh dear," she whispered and stepped out of Nash's arms as he placed her down, so her feet touched the floor. Eight sets of eyes rested on them.

He cleared his throat and flashed his executive staff a grin. "Who can keep a secret from my father for a thousand-dollar bonus?"

Clover darted a glance to Nash and shook her head. "Aren't you forgetting something, or shall I say, someone?"

He nodded and looked back to the still drop-jawed staff at the table. “Who can keep it from my father and Sally for two thousand? Raise your hands.”

Clover wanted to laugh as the hands shot up.

“Fantastic!” Nash clapped his hands together and chuckled. “Mine and Clover’s relationship stays in this room. Everyone enjoy your lunch and have a great weekend.” He turned and headed toward the door. “I know I will.”

Nash winked at the woman he was crazy about. It was going to be a great weekend indeed.

Chapter Twenty-Five

It had been over a week since Nash had dropped the bomb about Clover marrying someone else. Charlie sat in the clubhouse at the golf course drinking his beer when Mickey walked in. He looked just as down about things.

"You look about as happy as me," Charlie greeted, then sat and motioned to the bartender.

"My daughter hasn't returned my calls. When I talk to her, it's only for a few moments. She says she's busy. What the hell could she be doing at ten o'clock at night?"

"Something she should be doing with my son." Charlie didn't mean to sound bitter, but he was. For being a fantastic businessman, he was falling short when it came to his son.

Mickey scowled and sighed as the beer was set in front of him. "What are your spies over there saying?"

"Sally is still rattling about the rock on your daughter's finger that she showed up with on Monday. Martin says that things are fine, and so does Fritz. They've been busy, and no one's talking. I have no idea what's happening out there under the California sun. Suddenly, everyone, including my son, has decided that there is a job to do."

Mickey lifted his mug. "I'm sorry. I thought my Clover would be perfect for Nash."

Charlie shrugged and stared at the condensation on his mug. "Yeah, me too."

There was something not right about the whole situation in LA. Things were too quiet, and Nash wasn't doing anything in character. That thought alone bordered on scary. Why had Sally reported that he hadn't hit on any of the staff?

He even fired Julie. Things were not making sense.

His longtime friend shifted in his seat and faced the large television in the clubhouse. Charlie wasn't in the mood to watch television. He wanted to kick his son's ass. Maybe, he should have had Clover go to the office sooner when she went out. Not give her time to get to know anyone outside the office.

Mickey's hand hit his arm, and he glanced at Mickey, whose gaze was fixed on the screen. "Charlie!"

As he turned to the large flat screen, Charlie gasped and watched the commercial.

"You loved the sandwich as a kid; now enjoy the decadence of Lucky Ice Cream's peanut butter and banana ice cream. Smooth, creamy peanut butter ice cream with chunks of banana. Recapture your youth and your luck with Lucky Ice Cream."

Charlie was flabbergasted. "That's not one of

our flavors," he stammered. He knew this because he knew every flavor.

"Really? It sounds good," the bartender chimed in. Charlie and Mickey exchanged a look before both pivoted on their stools and turned to the bartender. "I think it sounds good." The young man's expression revealed his confusion. "If it's not one of the Lucky Ice Cream flavors, why a commercial for it?"

Charlie glanced at Mickey. "Is this your daughter's doing?"

"What about your son?"

"That boy is up to something. I told him to run the company, not get creative. I wonder what other flavors they've come up with. What else are they doing to my company?"

Mickey cast him a leveled look. "I didn't even know my daughter was seeing someone out in California. Now, she's engaged and hasn't even told her own mother. I have a good mind to fly out there and have a word with her."

"Well, from what I've been told, the guy spared no expense on her rock of a ring." Charlie stared at his good friend. "I thought she and Nash were a sure thing."

"You know, I think I'll fly out next Thursday night and surprise her at work on Friday."

Charlie smiled. "You know, I haven't been to LA in a couple years."

Oh yeah, it's time to visit my son.

"I'll go with you. If my son and your daughter

are up to something, you can bet I will find out."

Mickey lifted his beer. "Here's to outsmarting our kids."

Charlie lifted his glass. "And to the fact that they can't duck if they don't see us coming."

They raised their mugs and rattled against each other. Nash and Clover were in for one hell of a surprise.

Chapter Twenty-Six

Clover woke to find the door of the bedroom open. She didn't have to roll over to know Nash wasn't in bed with her. After clover climbed out from between the Egyptian cotton sheets, she grabbed the silk pajama top that went with Nash's bottoms. He never wore the thing anyway.

She covered her naked body and relished the feel of the expensive fabric against her skin. Clover may be a beach bum, but she was female, and silk was always good. Her bare feet left the soft carpet of the bedroom and touched the cold, expensive marble of the balcony.

Nash sat on the edge of one of the deck chairs, lost in thought and staring out at the skyline. The expensive cushion was dented from his weight.

It had been almost a week since they married. A detail Clover still hadn't told her family about. Nash seemed oblivious to her and continued to stare at the city.

Nash was so gorgeous. Hard to believe he was her husband. She quietly stepped closer, and his attention turned. His stressed features softened, and he smiled. "Are you okay?"

"I was going to ask you the same thing." She stepped closer and took in his bare solid chest.

He looked at her hand with her ring and gently took it in his. Nash studied the three-karat diamond princess cut stone. He pulled gently, and she sat next to him. "I was thinking."

Oh dear, please, Nash, don't regret us.

"I see." She wasn't sure where this conversation was going, and a small trickle of insecurity ran down her spine for someone usually confident.

Nash stared into her eyes, and his fingers played with the ring on her finger. "I like being married to you."

Not what she was expecting, but sweet. "I like being married to you, too."

He sighed. "Our keeping it a secret is already wearing on me. I want to wear a ring."

She blinked. "I bought you a ring, and you told me—"

"I know. I look at it every morning, Clover. It should be on my finger, not in a box." He sighed. "My father is pissed you're with someone other than me."

"You and I know the truth. Okay, and most of our executive staff also know the truth."

He chuckled. "I still can't believe I gave bonuses. I heard Martin out and out lie to Sally. He swore up and down you had the ring before the weekend. He even got Fritz to back it up." He hung his head.

"Nash, what is it?"

He glanced back at her. "You work hard at the office. You bring it home with you and work on trying to fix the mess I got the company into. You've actually got me working on something other than you. You're smart and funny. Half the time, we don't see much of each other at work unless we hunt the other down. Then we're usually interrupted."

She shook her head, still unsure where all this was going. "You're babbling."

"I'm hesitating. There's a difference."

Clover rubbed her eyes. She wasn't following Nash. "About? If it is about work…."

"Not about work, sweetheart." He released her hand and stood, then started pacing.

Sexy as hell in nothing but black silk pajama bottoms.

He shoved his hands through his hair and blinked at her. His muscular chest and shoulders rippled, as did his defined abdominal muscles. She grew wet between her legs and stood a few feet away from him.

"I know we have done everything else backward, but somewhere along the way, I fell in love with you."

She smiled at him and stepped closer. "How is this a bad thing?"

"Because I like you being in the office, even when we don't see each other. I like how we talk for hours and make grilled cheese at three in the morning, like last night." He sighed. "I don't want to be married for the sake of a baby. I love you and want a real marriage."

I love him, too.

"Nash, you and I both knew from the beginning that this was more of an arrangement."

He nodded and glanced away. Running his tongue over his teeth, he rested his hands on his hips. "I know, but you wanted to know what I was thinking." The heaviest sigh she'd ever heard left his firm lips and moved his entire torso.

I so want to make him sweat. He is always so arrogant and confident.

He wasn't now, and Clover knew he'd meant every word he said. She closed the distance between them and stood right in front of him. Clover forced herself not to smile. "Nash, I'm glad you told me how you feel."

Don't smile, no laughing.

He nodded and smiled weakly.

"I guess I should have told you three days ago, when I realized it, that I love you."

His weak smile faded. "You knew three days ago?"

"I think a little longer, but I was in denial," she confessed and shrugged her shoulders.

"You're in love with me?" He sounded unsure of himself. It was cute. Maybe he wasn't so tough after all.

"Yeah." She couldn't fight the grin a second longer and laughed.

Nash scowled and then broke out in a chuckle. "You had me worrying."

She giggled again. "And I was savoring every moment of it."

He reached out and wrapped her in the warmth of his strong arms. His features became serious. "I never thought it would be like this."

In all honesty, neither had she, not even for a second. "I wouldn't trade us for the world."

"I honestly think I knew I was in love with you when you literally climbed on the boardroom table to look at Martin's sandwich." His hands splayed across her back and clutched the fabric. "You're wearing my pajama top."

She smiled wickedly and stepped out of his arms. She pulled the hem up over her head and tossed it at him. Standing fully nude in front of him, she turned. "I don't need it."

She made it as far as the soft carpeting of the bedroom when Nash's footsteps came up behind her, and his strong arms caught her at the back and behind the knees. Lifting her off the ground, he was beside the bed in two strides and dropped her on the soft mattress covered in a plush duvet.

In the moonlight, though she couldn't see the desire in his eyes, she could feel it over her body as intensely as if it were his hands. He slipped his pajama bottoms off, and his large cock sprung to life. He slid his body over her. His erection glided over the sensitive skin of her inner thigh. "I do love you," she whispered.

Nash's hand gently brushed her hair off her cheek. "I love you." His lips came down hard against her mouth and his dick pressed against the wet folds between her legs. Slick already with need, she spread herself wider for him. Groaning, he entered her while his tongue thrust into her mouth. She bucked her hips against him and lifted her arms around his neck.

His tongue explored her mouth while she met his thrusts with the rhythmic rock of her hips. He lifted his lips from hers and positioned himself on his knees between her. Nash placed his hands behind her knees. He was glorious. With every thrust, the moonlight caught the ripple of his strong abdominal muscles.

She reached up and caressed his thigh to the tight, firm sinew of his ass. His thrusts picked up momentum, and the pressure across her stomach built. He slipped a hand to a breast and gently played with the nipple between his strong fingers.

The erotic gesture was all she needed. Her pussy clamped around Nash, and her body shook. Clover's whole body trembled from the climax. A primal groan left him as he thrust hard and deep. His cock pulsed as his orgasm released hot and fast inside of her. She couldn't breathe as her lungs wouldn't take in air.

Nash's sweat-soaked chest slid against her naked body, and his cheek rested against hers. Her hand lightly touched his hair, savoring everything about the man she was sure she would never let go of. She would be pregnant in no time at the rate they were going.

The weirdest part was, for the first time, she really didn't mind giving up her old life for the one she was quickly building with Nash.

Chapter Twenty-Seven

The days were flying by too fast, in Nash's opinion. However, he couldn't really complain. He'd had a fantastic weekend, which included being taught to surf by his wife. They had also worked out a chance to set up a kiosk with free samples of the new peanut butter and banana ice cream.

It was a huge success.

Of course, they didn't know until Monday night when he and Clover finished reviewing the survey statistics.

His wife loved him, the sex was the best of his life, and the commercial response was good to the new flavor. Life was perfect. He had even convinced Clover to come in early to work with him Tuesday morning.

"Why such a funny smile?" she asked as they rode the elevator up to the offices.

He turned to Clover and chuckled before he kissed her lips. "Don't be mad."

His wife rolled her eyes and cast him a worried expression. "Okay, you've never started a sentence like that before. That's not a good sign.

Chances are I'm going to get mad."

He withdrew his hand from his pocket and showed her his hand. "I really want this."

Her features softened as she studied the gold band on his finger. She glanced from his hand to meet his gaze. "How can I be mad at you for that?"

She stretched up, kissed his lips, and turned back to the elevator doors as she took his hand in hers.

"I just worry about you," she confided as the elevator doors opened and she stepped back into the foyer at reception. "I didn't think we would tell anyone we were married until we told our families."

Nash was about to speak when Sally rose from behind the desk wide-eyed.

"Oh sweet fucking hell," he breathed in horror.

"Nash?"

He released Clover's hand and gently captured her by the shoulders before he turned her around to see a slack-jawed Sally.

"Oh, dear!" She stepped backward and smacked right into his chest.

Sally narrowed her gaze on them to the point she looked like she was squinting. "I knew something was going on," she scolded with a finger wag. "Nashville O'Leary, are you keeping something from me?"

He was about to answer, but she held her hand up as if to signal him to stop. She glanced at Clover, then looked back at him.

"Sally..." he started but wasn't sure what to say.

"Don't Sally me. Your father has had a real bee in his bag since he discovered that Ms. Callaghan had a ring on her finger." She looked to Clover. "So, you reeled him in?"

Clover cleared her throat and stepped forward. "Could you rephrase that, please?"

Nash wasn't sure if Clover was mad or upset, but he didn't want her to be either. Sighing, he turned to Sally. "What exactly do you mean by that?"

She smiled warmly, and her expression revealed she was genuinely happy. "The moment I discovered who Clover was and spoke to her, I knew she was just the woman to tame you. She actually called me an ass-kiss."

"No, she didn't?" Nash tried not to sound sarcastic but failed mildly.

"Yes, and when I realized this young lady had spunk, I thought, good. That's what that boy needs." She wagged her finger again. "Why doesn't your father know?"

"Oh hell." Clover all but whimpered the two small words.

"Wait!" Sally stopped Nash again. "Answer me this first. Are you two married because I am quite sure that's what I heard?"

Well, at least he could wear his ring. The whole world would know he and Clover had married now that Sally knew. "Yes, Clover and I are married. No, my father doesn't know, and neither does hers. We're hoping to keep it from them a little longer. They kind of set us up, and...."

She smiled. "Say no more. Contrary to popular belief, I can keep a secret." She glanced at Clover, and her smile broadened as she snatched up Clover's hand and stared at the ring. Sally giggled and fanned herself, then turned to Nash. "You're a nice-looking couple."

"And you won't tell?" his wife asked, sounding more like a little girl than the executive she was.

"You know, I swear, Charlie O'Leary is a control freak and set his expectations low for our Nash. You brought out what he was capable of and settled his less than chaste ways." Sally hugged her quick and nodded at Nash. "You did well, so don't mind me."

Sally turned and strode toward her desk. She stopped and turned back around. "By the way, Mr. O'Leary, that's a wonderful tie."

Nash fought back the laugh and reclaimed his wife's hand in his own. Yep, it was a Tuesday.

Chapter Twenty-Eight

By Friday, Clover was relieved things had gone well with Sally, and almost all of the executive staff had seen Nash's ring. It was an unspoken rule that no one mentioned it to Charlie. He had called a couple times, and for once, Sally was telling Clover and Nash about Charlie instead of it being the other way around. She was a spy turned ally and was quickly becoming a friend to Clover.

"I think we should come up with another flavor or two," Nash told the casually dressed executive staff that sat around the boardroom table at their morning meeting.

"We were debating about adding a peanut butter and jam version," Everett, the product executive, informed them.

"Jam sounds really good, especially on a toasted bagel with cream cheese," Fritz agreed as he exchanged a nod with Martin.

"Clover, what do you think?" Nash asked.

"Jam is good."

Yep, definitely with cream cheese.

"I actually had a crazy idea," Fritz spoke up.

"See, honey, you are contagious." Nash spun

in his chair and winked at her. Chuckles erupted around the table.

Clover rolled her eyes and smiled at Fritz. “There are no crazy ideas. What’s your idea?”

“I remember when my wife was pregnant; she craved pickles and ice cream.”

“Apparently, that’s a common craving,” Nash chimed in and waved his hand, encouraging the other man to continue.

Clover hid her smile. She and Nash had checked out baby websites lately and had bought a couple books. He was definitely a reader, fascinated with the process. “So, what’s your idea, Fritz?” she encouraged.

“What if we had a pickle-flavored ice cream?”

“My daughter craved pickles and ice cream when pregnant with my granddaughter.” Another executive, Dennis, spoke up. He chuckled. “Her birthday is tomorrow.”

“She was born on St. Patrick’s day?” Martin asked. “How lucky is that? You’re Irish, right, Dennis?”

“Yeah, there’s going to be a big party for her tomorrow at our house. She’ll be five.”

Clover shook her head. “I forgot St. Patrick’s Day is tomorrow.” She turned back to Fritz. “I like the idea of the pickle-flavored ice cream.” She turned to the product executive. “Everett, is it possible to—” Her words stopped as her brain caught up to the processed information. “It’s the sixteenth?”

"All day," Martin replied with a smile.

Oh my God!

She turned to Nash

The boardroom door opened, and Sally flew over the threshold. "Mr. O'Leary, sorry to interrupt, but we have a small problem."

Nash stared at the elderly secretary, playing with the end of the pen over his lips. "Sally, what's wrong?"

"I'm late," Clover spit out.

Nash turned and looked at her. "For what?"

"Your father is here," Sally gulped, "and heading down the hallway here."

Clover shook her head, stood up, and blinked. "No, Nash, I'm two days late." She hadn't meant it to be a public announcement, but she was slightly stunned. She had never been late in her life.

Well, not until now. Oh, my god, now what? Am I…?

All eyes turned to her. Nash tossed the pen, spun in his chair, and then blinked at her. "Are you sure? The fourteenth of February." He answered his own question and stood.

"Oh dear," Sally breathed.

"Nashville!" Charlie barked, causing Clover to turn to the door.

"Oh hell!" she whispered as she glanced at her father standing next to him. She darted a dread-filled expression to Nash.

"Clover Callaghan!" Her father called calmly—too calmly. "I need to have a word with you."

"I'm sorry, she's in a meeting, and it'll have to wait." Sally stepped in front of him. "Can I show you a comfy chair and get you something to drink while you wait?"

Her father glared at Sally. "No, I need to speak to my daughter now." There it was in his tone.

Pure temper.

"This could get ugly," Nash whispered. They exchanged another edgy look. He smiled. "No stressing, okay?" His voice was just a breath, but she had heard him. She nodded as they both glanced back to their fathers.

Charlie started toward the table. "Nashville!"

Clover grabbed her purse and darted a glance to where Sally was arguing with her father. She had the most terrible urge to cry but met Fritz's gaze as he pointed to the boardroom door. She checked to see where Charlie was, to discover him standing over by Nash.

Martin stood up and blocked his view of Clover. "Mr. O'Leary, it is so nice to see you."

Carefully, she stepped away from the table but had to get past her dad and Sally. "Mickey, get over here!" Charlie called, surrounded by staff members that had taken Martin's cue. Her father broke away and stomped over to where Charlie stood with Nash.

Clover hurried by them, and Sally waved a hand as she quietly pulled open the door with her other hand. Clover slipped over the threshold, and Sally followed her, leaving the men behind.

"I have to go to the doctor," Clover whimpered. Her heart was racing, and tears hit her lashes. She stopped in front of the elevator, and Sally studied her.

Concern etched itself in the older woman's features. "Do you want me to go with you?"

She shook her head and again resisted the urge to cry. "I want Nash."

Sally winked. "I'll tell him you're at the doctor's and get him to meet you there."

Clover nodded as the elevator doors opened, and she stepped on. "Sally." She turned at met the secretary's gaze. "I'm scared."

"I had three. There's nothing to be scared of until they become teenagers." She laughed as the elevator doors closed.

"Wonderful, what a reassuring thought," she whispered as the elevator lowered her closer to the doctor and further away from Nash.

Chapter Twenty-Nine

Nash couldn't believe the chaos that ensued in a matter of moments. His life had spun out of control. More than being surprised by his father showing up was the fact his wife was late. He had lost track of her as she had slipped out the door with Sally. As if he had conjured her up, Sally appeared back at the boardroom door and nodded at him.

"You have a call, Mr. O'Leary, on line one."

His father spun around. "Who is it? Tell them I'll call them back."

Sally crossed her arms over her chest and looked sternly over her glasses at his father. "*Not* you, sir, your son."

Nash nodded and picked up the phone. "Nashville O'Leary."

"Nash, it's me," Clover whispered.

Clover, thank God!

"I just wanted to let you know I am heading to Dr. Hamilton's office."

He couldn't tip anyone off who was on the other end of the phone. More than anything, he wanted to be with Clover. Never was she going to go through any of this alone. "I'll look after that immediately," he told her, not wanting to raise any red flags with anyone around the room.

"Where the hell did that flighty daughter of mine go?" Mickey roared in a temper.

"I'll meet you there," Nash whispered and hung up the phone. He stared at Mickey, and the room fell silent. "Your daughter had an appointment."

"Fine then!" his father barked. "Everyone out, so I can talk to my son."

He ignored his father for the moment. "No disrespect, Mr. Callaghan, but I would really appreciate it if you didn't call Clover flighty." He didn't mean to sound terse, but her father, possibly his, didn't want to see Nash's protective streak.

"Nash, that's no way to speak to Mickey!" his father bellowed.

"Time to leave!" Martin called as he and the rest of the board filed towards the door, almost at a run.

"I'll call my daughter whenever I see fit!" Mickey fumed as everyone left the room, and Nash walked over to the door of the boardroom that closed shut.

"Not around me, you won't. If you don't mind, Dad, Mickey, I have to see my wife." He reached for the handle.

"You got married!" his father stammered. "First Clover gets engaged. Now we find out you got married." He exchanged a bleak and ashen expression with Mickey, then looked back at Nash. "Just who the hell did you marry?"

Nash pulled open the door and grinned, flipping a finger to Mickey. "His daughter."

He walked out the door and left the two fathers silent. Hurrying down the hall toward the elevator, he had officially had enough bullshit from both fathers and their crazy antics. Right now, he wanted Clover. He pushed the button and struggled to keep his composure.

"Good luck, Mr. O'Leary."

"Thanks, Sally."

"Not so fast, Nashville," his father yelled as he and Mickey hurried down the hall. "You have some explaining to do."

Nash's final straw of patience snapped, and he stared at the two men. "Then I'll be explaining in the car."

Chapter Thirty

Clover paced the floor of Dr. Hamilton's waiting room. She had already talked to him and was thankful he could see her on such short notice, despite being nervous and unsure what to expect. Still, Clover couldn't believe she was again here but without Nash. She thought of her husband and how she had left him with her dad and Charlie at the office. She could only imagine the chaos and the questions.

"It will be okay," the secretary told her sweetly.

"I'm not worried," she replied.

Okay, that was just a big fat lie. It's not okay. I want my husband.

The office door opened behind her, and she glanced at the threshold. Her heart almost stopped when Nash smiled and walked over to her. "Nash."

He set his hands gently on her hips and brushed her mouth with a soft kiss. "Have you gone in yet?"

"Just waiting." She blinked. "It might be too early to tell." Clover glanced to the other two men standing there, and she darted a stressed expression at Nash. "I don't want to argue."

"Clover," her father started and walked over to her. "Nash explained everything on the way. You do know that your mother is going to kill you, right?"

"Thanks, Dad." Her stomach rolled. As if this whole situation wasn't stressful enough, now she had her dad and Nash's father to contend with on top of everything.

"How are you?" Charlie asked with a smile.

"Fine." She turned to Nash. "Nervous. I'm really nervous."

"Everything is going to be fine," he assuredly offered a sweet smile.

"Mr. O'Leary, I'm glad you could make it." Dr. Hamilton greeted them with a smile. "I'm glad you took my advice."

Nash chuckled. "Yeah, I guess you can say I did."

"You and..." He glanced at Clover's hand and broadened his grin as he focused back on Nash. "You and your wife can step into my office."

Clover stepped forward.

"Not without us!" her father called as he and Charlie stepped closer to her and Nash.

"And who are you, people?" Dr. Hamilton asked with a lack of amusement coating his words.

"We're their fathers," Charlie explained.

Dr. Hamilton bounced his attention from Nash to Clover and back. "It's up to you, but they will have to stand."

"Nash?" She looked to her husband, who took

her hand in his.

"You realize we will never hear the end of this end as it is, right?" Nash turned to the two older men looking more like schoolboys up to mischief than they did possible grandfathers. "You better behave," he warned them and led Clover down the hall toward the office.

She sat down, and Nash sat next to her. The door shut, and she shot a look at the fathers. Nash squeezed her hand.

Dr. Hamilton cleared his throat. "I must say that I'm glad you kids have gotten married. You look good together."

"Thank you," Nash told the doctor. "Do you know if Clover is pregnant or not?"

The doctor nodded. "It's quite early, but going by your wife's medical history, I thought, why not?" He glanced at Clover. "Congratulations to you both."

"Oh my God, we did it!" She looked to Nash.

He stood and pulled her to her feet. "I love you." He looked so incredible and lowered his head to kiss her.

"I can't believe we lost the bet," her father called out.

Clover put her hand on Nash's chest and stopped him from kissing her. "You bet our fathers whether I was pregnant or not?"

He would have looked sheepish if he didn't look so damn sexy and happy. "I did. They didn't think you were."

She glanced quickly to where the fathers were, then to her husband again. "How did you know?"

"Luck of the Irish, baby."

She smiled at him. "That's *Sweetheart* to you. A baby is what we're having."

A wicked grin spread across his lips. "Maybe, but I'm getting kissed now." He lowered his mouth to hers and let go of her hand to wrap her in his arms. Nash's lips touched hers, and Clover knew she was lucky, in more than an ice cream sort of way, but a woman in love with her new life way.

About Kandi Silvers

Born and raised in Las Vegas, Nevada, I still call Sin City home. I've always been a sucker for romance novels and movies, especially romantic comedies. Writing is more than words; it captures slices of characters' lives and shares them with the reader. I firmly believe that heroes and heroines had a life before page one of any story and their past and life experiences made them who they are.

Coming from the southwest, I have a soft spot for cowboys, but I also love suspense, a bit of intrigue, and kick-ass heroines. Of course, there is always the time to slip in a good paranormal. I try to keep my writing diverse and always on the naughty side. Happy reading!

~Kisses,

Kandi

www.kandisilversauthor.com

www.ingramcontent.com/pod-product-compliance
Lightning Source LLC
LaVergne TN
LVHW010105170826
845678LV00012B/2251

* 9 7 9 8 8 4 7 6 0 7 6 8 1 *